The Misfits &

The Magic Stone

Written by M. A. Cope

Created by M. A. Cope & J. Brier

To honesty and friendship, may you always walk hand in hand.

The Magic Stone

There is a stone, a magic stone, within the witching world. The birth of every pure blood witch forges the stone, appearing beside the child as it lies in its crib for the first time. Formed from the four elements—earth, air, fire and water—the stone is the source of a witch's power as they learn their craft. As each witch grows and develops so the stone becomes smaller until it vanishes, the witch it was cast to raise having absorbed its power. Its disappearance heralds a witch's initiation into the Coven, imbuing the witch with both the proficiency to cast spells, but also the strength and wisdom to control them.

The magic stone brings life to everything around it. Its power is used by its witch to bring essence to their craft. Only witches can absorb, by osmosis, the potency of the magic stone. The magic stone must not be separated from its witch. If such an abhorrent situation should occur, the power within the stone would build and build, and with nowhere to go will eventually reach critical mass, the result being an explosion bringing death and destruction to everything around it.

It cannot be stressed enough that magic stones should never be separated from their magical owners… NEVER!

The witching world knows the magic stone as a Runial.

A Runial looks like a moonstone and is the size of a robin's egg. It is flat like a sea-hewn pebble and is milky-lilac in its resting colour with active swirls, as if it is constantly stirring. When activated, the swirls become a myriad of colours, each reflecting the virtues and sins all spells encompass:

RED - chastity and lust
PINK - abstinence and gluttony
YELLOW - liberality and greed
GREEN - kindness and envy
LIGHT BLUE - diligence and sloth
VIOLET - humility and pride
ORANGE - patience and wrath

With pride being the root of all sin and hence the deadliest, violet is the predominant colour of the Runial.

But the chemistry of spells isn't the only thing the Runial imbues its witch with. Focus, intent and concentration—FIC—are the defining strengths of all witches. Focus to shut out everything but what lays before, intent to follow through on that which they have committed to, and concentration on the spell itself, allowing the chemistry to work its magic. To help develop FIC, the witch must wear the Runial on a silver chain close to their heart, or at least that's where it should be. Meg Broom, however, finds the stone too heavy and keeps it in her backpack instead.

It is FIC most young witches struggle with, and you won't be surprised to learn Meg Broom is no exception...

Meg Broom

Witches are a rare and valued supernatural being. Once upon a time, they were the only *beings* able to live in the human world, blending seamlessly into the population. But their need to grow plants and herbs for their spellcasting, and their natural ability to heal the sick and the wounded, brought them to the attention of the powers that be, who frowned upon anyone not following the "right" path. As a result, the Cull ensued, wiping out most of the witches. Those that remained went underground.

Only the Brooms stood firm, refusing to be driven to constantly looking over their shoulders. Instead, they chose to move to the other side of The Wall, with all the other supernatural creatures. The Brooms were the only family to do so.

Meg Broom was a pure-blood witch, one of the last of her kind. She was the only witch in the entire school, apart from her aunt, Mrs Broom, and so the only child able to perform actual magic. Because of this, she was the envy of everyone and was in constant demand to perform. But, being young, Meg still had her training wheels on, her Runial her constant companion.

Meg was an only child, an accident as her parents liked to tell anyone who would listen. As such, they spent little time with her, instead focusing on their jobs at the Consulate, where they mediated and presided over laws governing the supernatural world. Forever being treated as "in the way", Meg sought solace in books, where she could be whoever she wanted to be and go wherever she wanted to go, with no one telling her otherwise. Her isolation, though, had its consequences, and Meg grew into a quiet, reserved child, who kept to herself and hid in the shadows.

Mrs Broom never approved of her brother's attitude to his only child and took Meg under her wing, hoping to show her the love and attention her parents didn't. But no matter how much time she spent with her, Meg remained locked in her own little world, a world Mrs Broom couldn't enter.

In an effort to draw her out, Mrs Broom consulted the Coven, and they agreed to allow Meg a *familiar*, although this wasn't usually permitted until initiation. As such, Ozzy the big black cat wandered into Meg's world one day, the whoop of joy and the grin on Meg's face being all the confirmation Mrs Broom needed to know she'd done the right thing. But instead of drawing Meg out into the world, Ozzy simply became the one she talked to, and she withdrew even further from Mrs Broom.

Once again, Mrs Broom consulted the Coven, and they granted her permission to give Ozzy the gift of speech; a gift Mrs Broom frequently wished she could retract, as the black cat was a rather opinionated familiar…

***

'Can you drop us off here please, Auntie Gert?' Meg asked as she glanced out of the car window at the leafy corner that preceded the road to school.

'Why ever would I do that, you silly girl? It's not much further.' Mrs Broom tutted as she waited for every single vehicle in sight to pass before she turned.

'Please,' Meg whispered, more to herself than anyone else.

Whether she heard her, Meg wasn't sure, but Mrs Broom pulled away without responding.

'You're doing it again, Gertie,' Ozzy piped up from his languorous position along the parcel shelf.

Mrs Broom slammed on the brakes, causing a cacophony of horns behind her, and whirled around.

'First of all, don't call me Gertie,' Mrs Broom snapped, narrowing her eyes at Ozzy, who simply mirrored her movements, before yawning and proceeding to lick his sun-warmed fur.

'Secondly, doing "what" again?'

'Treating Meg like her parents do,' Ozzy replied, fixing his yellow stare on Mrs Broom, her purple hair fizzing in response to her current state.

'I am not—'

'Of course you are. You are not listening to—'

'Ozzy, it's okay. Let's just do what we always do,' Meg said, reaching out to settle her familiar. The last thing she wanted was a row before school. She needed to brace herself for what was to come… what always came.

'No, it isn't okay, Meg. Gertie doesn't see what happens when she leaves you.'

'I told you not to… What happens when I leave you, Meg?' Mrs Broom asked, her attention deflected to her niece, concern edging her voice.

'Noth—'

'What do you think happens?'

'I don't know, Ozzy, that's why I'm asking Meg.' Mrs Broom glared at the black cat, but he just sat up tall and glared right back.

'Stop it, you two, honestly,' Meg muttered, rolling her eyes. This was all she needed.

'Tell me, Meg, maybe I can—'

'That's just it, Gerts. It's you that's the problem.'

'Ozzy! That's enough!' Meg said and swatted the cat on his nose. Ozzy merely shook his head and shrugged.

Meg chanced a look at her aunt to see her staring open-mouthed.

'I'm sorry for that, Auntie Gert, but he is kind of right.'

'But what have I done? I would never—'

'You haven't "done" anything. It's just that you're a teacher, and me being seen to arrive with a teacher is… well… let's just say it doesn't make me very popular.'

'But why on earth would you want to be popular?'

'Oh, dear Satan, woman, you are *so* missing the point.'

'Ozzy! Stop it,' Meg chastised.

'Well, she is,' Ozzy huffed, before turning his back on them both.

'There are times I wish I hadn't given that cat the—'

'He is right, though, Auntie, it's not about being popular.'

'Well, what is it then?'

'I just don't want them to see me at all.'

'Now, Meg, I—'

'Oi! You can't just stop at a junction, you stupid—'

But Mrs Broom didn't give the irate motorist time to finish insulting her, instead picking up her wand and waving it in his direction, never once turning from Meg. For her part, Meg swivelled her eyes to see the other driver soundlessly yelling at her aunt.

'Meg?'

Meg looked back at her aunt to find her pressing her lips together, the mole on her top lip trembling as she fought to keep the brimming tears from tumbling.

'Don't get upset, Auntie Gert. I just want to walk the rest of the way with Ozzy, that's all.' Meg reached out and brushed a stray tear from Mrs Broom's cheek.

Mrs Broom nodded and turned away, clearing her throat before saying, 'I understand. Would you like me to pick you up here too... after school?'

Meg looked into the rear-view mirror and met her aunt's gaze. 'Yes, please.'

Mrs Broom nodded again. 'Well, out you both get, then. I'm going to be late at this rate and that will never do. It's my job to catch the latecomers, not be one of them.'

Grinning from ear to ear, Meg scooped Ozzy off the parcel shelf, grabbed her backpack and jumped out of the car.

'See you later,' she said and blew her aunt a kiss.

***

'I told you it would work,' Ozzy said as Meg deposited him on the pavement. He stretched and shook out his fluffy fur, before falling in step with a now humming Meg.

'I know, but you don't have to be so rude to her. She's only looking out for me.'

'I look out for you. Gertie just...'

'Stop calling her Gertie, Ozzy. You know she hates it.'

'Why do you think I do it?'

Meg glanced down at her familiar and he shrugged.

'You're terrible. She's done a lot for me, so, for me, just tone it down, will you?'

'Hmmm, so what's the plan of entry today then, now that you've gone all covert?'

'It's hardly covert, is it? They're still going to see me coming.'

'And you think they'll leave you alone?'

Meg shrugged. 'I can hope.'

'Don't hold your breath,' Ozzy muttered as they reached the school gates.

Meg stopped.

Please leave me alone, please leave me alone, she willed as she stood staring at the kids milling around in the playground. She took a deep breath and stepped through the gates, Ozzy by her side as always.

'Here she comes. What, no lift this morning, Sabrina? In detention?'

Meg fixed her gaze and carried on walking, but an inconspicuous entrance was not to be, despite her precautions.

'Here!'

Meg stopped abruptly as a flower was thrust in front of her. She turned to a girl, much younger than her, twirling from side to side, her skin alternately swathed in fur and then bare, her ears morphing to pointed and back.

'Thank you,' Meg said, accepting the flower from the young werewolf. The girl scampered away, sniggering.

'Make it open, witch.'

Meg closed her eyes and shuddered at the sound of his voice. This is who she'd hoped to avoid.

'Jonas.'

'The very same. Now, I've chosen a much simpler task for you today. Surely, if you really are the witch everyone says you are, you'll be able to open a mere flower.'

'The fact you've picked this flower, so it is no longer living, makes that—'

'Don't want to hear your excuses, Broom. Do that hocus pocus and open the flower.'

'Jonas, it's not that simple, I—'

'Do it, or you're not getting any further.' Jonas stepped forward, looming over her, his height making her diminutive frame even smaller.

Meg stared up into the dark, hooded eyes of the most popular boy in school. He grinned his disarming grin that put so many in his thrall, his fangs glinting in the sunlight. Meg raised her eyebrows.

You don't charm me.

'Don't let him bully you,' Ozzy hissed.

'What's that fleabag meowing at, Broom?'

'Shh,' Meg said to Ozzy. 'He doesn't like confrontation, that's all,' she said to Jonas.

'Confrontation? There's no confrontation. We're all friends here, aren't we?' Jonas said, slapping his best friend Griff on the shoulder before gesturing to the assembling audience. 'It's about time the only witch in the school proved her mettle.'

'You don't have to do this, Meg,' Ozzy said.

'And shut that cat up, too. The mewling is pathetic.'

Meg felt Ozzy bristle and heard the growl erupt inside him. She placed a hand on his head, massaging his ear, his growl turning to a purr in an instant.

'Okay,' she said. 'Give me some space.'

Pursing his lips, Jonas nodded and flicked his hands for the crowd to move back; they obeyed without question.

Meg laid the flower on the grass, hoping its closeness to the earth would aid her, before removing her backpack. She unzipped it, rummaging inside until she found what she was looking for—her magic stone.

She nodded to Ozzy, who sat to the side, his bushy tail flicking back and forth as he turned to stare at Jonas through his slitted yellow eyes.

Meg stood with her feet planted wide, the magic stone between her palms as she circled them, warming the stone, revving up its power. Soon she felt the electricity as the stone sparked and she tried to focus her mind—FIC—on drawing the sputtering power into her body. She took a deep breath and visualised the white light from the stone entering her body through her palms, her aura glowing as it did so. Meg smiled, pleased with her progress.

'Why are we waiting…?' sang Jonas, causing his flock to giggle.

Meg felt her power cower and retreat, leaving her spinning on the spot, almost falling over as she failed to find anything to stop her whirling. Ozzy stepped in, and Meg wrapped her arms around him and buried her face in his thick fur.

'Deep breaths. Keep your eyes closed,' he murmured. 'It will pass. It always does.'

'Come on, Broom. I thought spells were Witch 101. You've done nothing except massage that rock. The poor flower will be dead before long.'

'The poor flower is dead anyway,' Meg muttered into Ozzy's fur.

She ventured to open her eyes, and when the world stayed where it was, she released Ozzy and stood up.

'Oooo, look, everyone, the witch is back for round two.' The crowd sniggered and Meg felt the tears well up inside her.

'Ignore him,' Ozzy said as he brushed against her. 'You can do this.'

'But that's just it. I can't. It's dead,' she whispered out of the side of her mouth.

'He doesn't know that. Just give him a show, that's all he wants.'

Meg looked up at Jonas, wishing with all her heart she could wipe the smug grin off his face, but Auntie Gert had forbidden her from using her magic to harm… more's the pity.

Instead, she closed her eyes and focused on the stone again, waiting until she felt the power flowing inside her, before she opened her eyes, fixing her gaze on the wilting flower.

'Oh, little flower close at hand,
Recall your connection to this land.
Draw from the earth the strength you need,
To open your petals and cast wide your seed.
As I do will, so mote it be.'

Silence reigned over the amassed crowd as they watched and waited. Meg used all of her willpower not to look away from the flower. FIC was the name of the game—focus, intent, concentration. Even though she knew it was hopeless—the flower being dead already—Meg willed it to move, just a flinch, so she could show Jonas who she was.

'Aren't you supposed to summon the Goddess or something?' snorted Jonas.

Meg closed her eyes without thinking, breaking the FIC, gritted her teeth and muttered, 'Not when I still have my training wheels on.' She squeezed the magic stone, but the damage was done. She opened her eyes in time to see the flower take its last breath and wilt.

'Ha, you killed it!' Jonas shouted, his flock following suit.

Meg felt the flush rise through her coffee-coloured skin, up into the roots of her spiralled, purple hair. She clenched her fists, the magic stone pulsating in her palm.

'Don't do it,' hissed Ozzy.

'No, you killed it when you picked it,' she hurled at Jonas. 'If you were as clever as you think you are, you'd know that!'

'What did you say to me, witch?' Jonas's face transformed and his followers stepped back.

'Meg,' Ozzy whispered, tugging at her arm, but Meg stood her ground. She planted her feet wide, rolled her shoulders back, closed her eyes, took a deep breath, then opened her eyes, tilting her head right back until she met Jonas's ominous glare.

'I said… if you are so clever, you'd know you killed the flower the minute you picked it.' She thrust out her chin to emphasise her point, but it had little effect when her head was so far backwards it almost touched her back.

'What did you say to me, witch?' Jonas repeated, grabbing Meg by the throat and lifting her off her feet.

Meg gripped the magic stone, muttering under her breath, but she couldn't focus as Jonas squeezed her windpipe.

Ozzy, on the other hand, had no problem in focusing, and launched himself at Jonas, clawing his way up his body.

'Oi, Griff, get this fleabag off me!' He shoved at Ozzy, his grip firm around Meg's neck, but Ozzy had buried his claws deep and no amount of Griff trying to extract him was going to change that. The only thing it did was cause Jonas to howl in pain, which kind of was the intention, although him releasing Meg was the desired outcome.

'Jonas Lee, unhand my niece this instant!' Mrs Broom's voice thundered across the playground, closely followed by a shaft of light. Jonas howled again, releasing Meg—who collapsed to the ground—before blowing on his now burning arm.

'What on earth is going on over here?' Mrs Broom demanded, gripping Jonas by the scruff of the neck and forcing him to look at her.

'N-n-nothing, Mrs Broom,' Jonas muttered. A few snickers could be heard from the amassed crowd, but a glare from Jonas soon silenced them.

'Meg?' Mrs Broom turned her attention to Meg, who was still slumped on the floor, massaging her neck. Ozzy had positioned himself between her and Jonas.

'Nothing, Auntie… Mrs Broom, it's fine,' she said and dropped her magic stone in her backpack before her aunt saw it.

'Well, it didn't look like nothing. Anyone else care to enlighten me as to what has been going on?' Mrs Broom turned to the masses, but everyone suddenly had something else to occupy their attention.

'Hmmm, well, it looks like you'll be in detention alone, Mr Lee,' she said, pursing her lips, and making her mole quiver.

'Ah, Mrs Broom, that's not fair. She is just as—'

'Are you trying to say my niece picked a fight with you?'

'Well…'

'Well, what?'

Jonas toed the ground before shrugging.

'I didn't think so. But, if you want some company, I'm sure Mr Fitzroy here will be only too happy to join you, won't you, Mr Fitzroy?' Mrs Broom turned her stare on Griff, who nodded, smiling, until Jonas rolled his eyes and Griff realised what he'd agreed to. Then his shoulders slumped, and he too toed the ground.

'Right then, given the bell rang a few moments ago, I suggest you all get to class. And I'll see you after school.' Mrs Broom released Jonas and waved her wand to propel him, and the rest of his flock, on their way.

'Are you going to tell me what happened?' Mrs Broom asked, turning back to Meg, who was zipping up her backpack and getting to her feet.

As she lifted her backpack to slip her arms into it, it caught on something. In no mood to find out what, Meg tugged. The backpack sprang loose, nearly toppling her, but she managed to stay upright.

'Nothing new,' she said and shrugged, before heading towards the school block, Ozzy in tow.

The Misfits

It was Achoo's favourite time of day—a break time; a time he could indulge in his favourite pastime—sleeping—with no interruptions. The sun was high in the sky and the day was lazy and warm, a feeling Achoo shared. As the Misfits trooped outside, Achoo zeroed in on his nap site. He detached himself from the group, hoping they didn't notice, and slunk off to the enormous boulder that occupied pride of place on the lawned area beside the playground.

Apparently, the boulder was a meteor that fell out of the sky one day, narrowly missing a student who was sunbathing at the time. Achoo was a tad dubious about this story, as the boulder wasn't buried in the ground at all. Instead, it appeared to have been placed... artistically. Surely, if it had fallen from space, then it would have left a vast crater? This was a puzzle Achoo always pondered when contemplating his boulder, as he liked to refer to it.

Achoo yawned. Thinking made him even more sleepy. Whilst he had made inroads into sleeping less, to please his dad—the Alpha—Achoo made up for it when his dad wasn't around. It wasn't his fault he liked to sleep, was it?

The trouble was, since he controlled, to a certain extent, his wolfing out, he was never as sleepy, so he often spent the time in what he liked to call a semi-conscious state, where he wasn't really asleep, but nor was he awake. He was in some kind of suspended animation where, to be frank, it could go either way. The warmth of the sun certainly helped push him towards sleep, but if a cloud passed over, increasing the shade from the boulder, it dragged him away from the land of Nod.

Achoo shrugged. He didn't care whether he fell asleep. The mere act of lying down and closing his eyes was enough for him to enjoy his favourite past-time.

***

It was Mina's favourite time of day—a break time; a time she could indulge in her favourite pastime—dreaming—with no interruptions. She angled her face to the sun, turning it from side to side, savouring the warmth as it penetrated her skin, knowing her mother would comment on the darkening of her freckles after school, like she did every day. Mina smiled. The gaps in her teeth where her prosthetic fangs should be allowed the breeze to tickle the roof of her mouth, making her giggle. If her mother could see her now, she'd be horrified.

Mina snorted as she rummaged in her pocket to make sure the fangs were still there. As long as she put them back in before she left school, her mother would never know.

She surveyed the lawn for the best place to daydream and saw Achoo slink behind his boulder. Mina glanced to the right and saw the cherry tree was vacant of visitors and headed over. She liked to lie under the tree; her legs up against the trunk, her gaze focused on the branches, hypnotised by their ebb and flow as they moved on the breeze. It was the perfect storm for a daydream.

Mina strode over to cop a squat beneath the cherry tree, emptying her backpack of her books, pencils and sketch pad, and spreading them out, hoping to deter anyone from joining her. She took her shoes off and lay down, resting the soles of her feet against the bark, and closed her eyes, focusing on connecting herself with the tree. As she felt the frizzle of energy, Mina allowed her gaze to travel upwards, concentrating on the cobalt sky periodically visible through the undulating branches. Her vision soon blurred and her mind drifted off, a goofy smile spreading across her face as her hands wafted with her imagination.

***

It was Zoe's favourite time of day—a break time; a time she could indulge in her favourite pastime—skating—with no interruptions. As soon as they exited the school building, Zoe bent forward, angled her body and pushed off, without a care for who may be about to cross her path. Luckily, there was no one. She raced around the playground, weaving in and out of the other kids, whooping and yelling as if she'd been locked up for a very long time. For Zoe, being still for more than five minutes was too much.

Keen to feel the breeze cooling her rotting flesh, Zoe focused and set about doing circuits of the playground, each one faster than the one before. She liked to break her speed record from the previous day, and usually she did okay, but yesterday had been carnage. The Bay twins hadn't been paying attention and had wandered into her path. She'd screamed for them to move, but as usual, they were away with the fairies and hadn't heard her.

The result? Well, let's just say, Zoe didn't have enough duct tape to put herself back together. Mina had come to the rescue, having taken to carrying tape in her own backpack, just in case her friend needed it. Zoe's mum, however, was incensed and grounded Zoe, which wasn't an issue, as Zoe didn't tend to go anywhere. The issue had been the confiscation of her favourite item—her roller blades.

Zoe grinned as she remembered sneaking into the pantry

that morning and climbing the shelving to find the hiding place her mum always used. Having retrieved her blades, she'd made a hasty exit. She knew her mum would be mad, especially as she always walked Zoe to school, but she should know better than to take away her blades.

Zoe made her body as tight and small as she dared, without dislodging a limb, narrowed her eyes to stop her left eyeball falling out, and leaned into her skating. Today she would break a record; she had no doubt.

***

It was Boo's favourite time of day—a break time; a time he could indulge in his favourite pastime—chatting—with no interruptions. Boo knew his friends wouldn't entertain interruptions, each wanting to indulge in their own favourite past times, so he needed to seek an alternative audience. The trouble was, today, the playground was pretty empty. Boo's heart sank. There was no one for him to talk to, and he needed to chat with someone; he'd explode otherwise.

He stood in the middle of the playground and looked around. He could try to get Zoe's attention, but the only way to do that would be to block her path. Being a ghost, he knew she couldn't hurt him, but she could have a nasty fall… again… and he didn't think that was a good idea, not after yesterday. Thinking of the previous day, Boo searched for the Bay twins, as they were always good to talk to, hanging on his every word, but they were nowhere to be seen.

Maybe they're still in the infirmary?

Yesterday had been quite nasty… blood everywhere… body parts everywhere. Zoe had been the easy one to put back together. He knew the twins would heal quickly—werewolves always did—but still… Boo wrinkled his nose and, hearing a tinkling giggle, he turned to see Mina lying beneath the cherry tree, her hands swiping at unseen things in the air. Boo shook his head.

Got a screw loose, that one.

He pondered going over and trying to engage her in conversation, but he'd tried that before. Mina had an uncanny knack for being able to block him out, which only made him try harder. But it never worked. Boo hated being ignored.

Ah, I know where everyone is.

Boo looked towards the sports field, and sure enough, there was Jonas holding court. The entire school had heard about the episode that morning and how Jonas felt he was being punished unfairly.

No doubt he's inciting a rebellion against Mrs B.

Boo shrugged. Jonas wouldn't get far with that. Nothing got past Mrs B. The thought of the morning's trouble prompted Boo to search the vicinity for Meg. He knew she wouldn't be at the sports field, but nor had he seen her inside. He wandered to the far end of the playground and, sure enough, sitting alone on one swing sat Meg Broom, her head bowed as she stroked her black cat. Boo wrinkled his nose. He didn't like cats. He used to, but since he'd adopted a rather flimsier form, cats tended to walk right through him, which made him uncomfortable. At least Zoe had been there to distract the old lady's black and white cat when they visited the other side of The Wall.

Having decided that spending time with Meg's cat wasn't worth the benefit of chatting, Boo turned to the boulder on the lawn and grinned.

He knew exactly who he'd annoy, conversation or not.

The Misfits Meet Meg Broom

'Ay ay, what you up to, Wolfie?' Boo said as he loomed over Achoo's inert form.

Achoo opened one eye, shielding it from the glare of the sun which passed through Boo's translucent form. 'Sleeping, what do you think?' he mumbled and closed his eye again, rolling over, his back to Boo.

'If you were sleepin' you wouldn't be talkin' now, would you?' Boo attempted to nudge Achoo with his foot, but as he wasn't concentrating hard enough, it passed right through, knocking Boo off balance.

'Go 'way,' Achoo muttered.

'I would, but I don't 'ave no one else to yarn to, so you're up, Wolfie.' Boo lay on the ground beside Achoo and stared up at the clouds. 'Why do you sleep so much, any'ow?'

'Coz I like it.'

'Waste o' time, if you ask me. I don't sleep at all, so I never miss 'owt.'

'Hmmm,' Achoo murmured, then yawned.

'Aw, come on, I'm bored. It's okay for you lot. You amuse yourselves, if that's what you call this, but me? I likes to 'ave a chinwag. You all know this, but you never want to chat…' Boo let the sentence hang and glanced at Achoo. The steady rise and fall of his ribs showed he'd fallen asleep.

Great! Now I send 'em to sleep!

Boo's hand was toying with the grass, which needed a cut, his fingers discovering the length, making him grin.

I know 'ow to wake 'im up!

Boo closed his eyes and scrunched his face up, concentrating his mind on the blade of grass now between his fingers. It took several attempts, but finally he pulled it from the ground. He held it high, twirling it before turning towards Achoo. Supporting himself on his elbow, Boo leaned over and danced the blade of grass across Achoo's nostrils, pulling his hand back as Achoo swiped at the annoyance.

It didn't take long before Boo's agitation had the desired effect and Achoo's body heaved as he got ready to sneeze. Boo moved out of the way and waited for the show. Soon enough, a slumbering Achoo, not in control of his senses, erupted into a fit of sneezing, wolfing in and out as he did so.

Boo doubled over with laughter.

'You think that's funny, do you?' Exhausted, Achoo lay flat on his back, panting, and stared up at Boo.

'Yeah, pretty much,' Boo said, and shrugged. 'I told you I was bored.'

'Haven't you two got anything better to do?'

The boys turned to see Mina striding over to them, belongings safely back in her backpack.

'Uh oh, she's got that look,' Achoo hissed.

'What look?' asked Boo.

'You'll see.'

'Well, I asked you a question?' Mina prompted when both boys remained gawping at her.

'You can't talk, Fangless. It's not like you've been studyin' for MENSA, is it?' Boo said.

'I am always doing something productive,' Mina retorted, her nose in the air.

'Yeah right,' Boo snorted. 'So, lyin' on your back, gigglin' and wavin' your 'ands at nuffin counts as, 'ow did you put it… productive"?'

'Yes, well, I have been doing other things too.'

Achoo raised his eyebrows at this and Mina had the good grace to blush, knowing she'd been caught out in a fib.

She cleared her throat before she said, 'Have you seen Meg? She looks a bit upset.'

'Well, she did have a run-in with Jonas this morning,' Achoo said, pushing himself up, his wolfing out under control.

'She has a run-in with Jonas and his sidekick every day, but I've never seen her upset before.'

'Well, go an' ask 'er if you're so concerned.'

Mina glared at Boo. 'You ask her. You're the one who likes to chat, remember.'

'Nah, not while that fleabag is with 'er.'

'What have you got against cats all of a sudden?' Mina asked.

'I ain't got no problem. It's them.'

'But, the old lady's cat never bothered—'

'Take it from me, Wolfie, me and those of the feline persuasion tend not to get on.'

'Oh, you mean they ignore you?' Mina said, raising her eyebrows.

Boo swallowed his retort. Some people would never understand the perils of being a ghost. ''Ow about getting Skater Girl to go talk to 'er?'

'Ha!' Achoo grunted. 'Good luck with stopping her. Don't you remember what happened yesterday?'

'Oh, she'll run out of steam soon. She always does,' Mina said with authority as she consulted her watch. 'In fact, if my calculations are correct, it should be any… minute… now.'

All three of them looked towards the playground to see Zoe suddenly pull herself upright and stop pushing forwards, allowing her momentum to slow.

As though she felt their gazes on her, Zoe turned and waved, changing direction and heading towards them. As she hit the grass, her blades stopped, and she toppled forward, righting herself, but ending up running towards her three friends.

'Form a line, quickly. Backs to her,' Mina ordered.

Achoo jumped to attention, standing beside Mina as they both braced for impact. Boo watched in fascination as an out-of-control Zoe ploughed into the two friends, sending them all toppling to the ground.

Boo stood over them, scratching his chin as he stared at the intertwined body parts. Zoe's were easy to identify as they were no longer attached to her body.

'Er, why didn't you stop before 'ittin' the grass?' he asked.

'Easier said than done,' Zoe replied, easing herself out of the knot with her intact arm. 'Can you grab my arm, please?' she asked as she retrieved her left foot.

'Boo has a point, Zoe. It's about time you learned to come to a halt. We won't always be there for you, you know,' Mina chastised as she opened her backpack and pulled out an enormous roll of duct tape.

'Not sure I want to keep doing this, even if we are,' grumbled Achoo, massaging his arm as he pulled it from beneath Mina.

'Oh, stop complaining. Of course, we'll be there for her. That's what friends are for... isn't it?' Mina glared at Achoo, who eventually shrugged and nodded.

'This is something you need to learn too,' she said, directing her attention to Boo. 'If you want to keep hanging around with us, that is.'

''Ey, that's a bit below the old belt, Fangless.'

'Stop calling me that! I have fangs now.'

'You don't wear them, though, do you?' Zoe commented.

'Well, no, not here, but… anyway, stop changing the subject. Boo, you need to step up when we need you, like just now. Maybe we wouldn't have fallen if you'd joined in.'

'Or maybe she'd 'ave passed right through me.'

'I thought you'd mastered that?' Zoe said and flinched as Mina forced her arm back in its socket.

'Hold this,' Mina directed Achoo. Achoo did as commanded, so Mina could secure Zoe's arm in place. 'Can you do the rest?' she asked Zoe.

'Yep. So, Spirit Boy, what happened to you being able to "solidify" yourself then?'

'It's a comin'. Can't rush these fings, you know.'

The friends lapsed into silence, watching, fascinated, as Zoe swiftly secured her ankle and scanned for other loose parts.

'So, what's with Meg?' Zoe asked, looking up to see the other three gawping at her. 'Okay, show's over, you can stop staring now, it's creepy.'

'Dunno,' said Achoo.

'Something's different,' Mina said.

'Why don't we just go an' ask 'er?' Boo suggested.

'I said that earlier, but you wouldn't,' Mina said.

'Correctomundo, and I wasn't puttin' meself forward now, merely suggestin' one of us should.'

'I think we all should,' Zoe said, standing up and wobbling on her blades.

'Does it never cross your mind to take those off, Skater Girl?'

'And what would I wear on my feet then?'

Without waiting for an answer, Zoe picked her way across the grass towards the swings and Meg. The others trooped after her.

Meg's Loss

'Oh, Ozzy, what am I going to do? Auntie Gert is going to kill me.' Meg wiped her eyes with her damp handkerchief before blowing her nose. The sound was like a trumpet.

'It'll turn up, don't worry,' Ozzy said, nuzzling Meg's hand until she stroked his head.

'How is it going to turn up? We've looked everywhere. You know I'm supposed to wear it.'

'So, why don't you then, if it's that important?'

'You know why. It's too heavy. Plus, everyone can see it if I wear it.'

'But if you'd been wearing it, you wouldn't have lost it.'

'Thanks a lot. I thought you were on my side.'

'I am. Just stating a fact.'

'Stating the obvious, you mean, as always,' Meg grumbled.

'Well, someone needs to point things out to you. Maybe you'll listen now.'

'We have to find it first.'

'Find what?'

Meg and Ozzy jumped at the sound of Mina's voice.

'Oh, hey, Mina… hey guys,' Meg said, sniffing and stuffing her handkerchief out of sight before sitting up straight and plastering a smile on her face.

'Her Runial,' Ozzy said, and yawned.

'Ozzy!'

'Well, there's no point in keeping it a secret. I thought you wanted to find it.'

'I do, but—'

'A what?' Boo interrupted.

'Oh, for goodness' sake, I thought you were one of us. Don't you know anything?' Mina said, exasperated.

'Whoa, wind your neck in, Fangless. We're not all walkin' dictionaries, you know.'

'Her magic stone,' Zoe volunteered as she pushed past Boo, who was keeping his distance, a watchful eye on Ozzy.

'What's a—'

'It's where she gets her power, you know, while she's learning,' Achoo said, nudging Boo closer.

'I'll stay 'ere, thanks,' Boo said, and stepped back again. ''Ow come she don't 'ave powers like we do?'

'Who *is* this heathen?' Ozzy said and stood up, prompting Boo to take another step back. 'Afraid of me, are you?'

'Nah, not afraid,' Boo said, fidgeting.

'Then come closer and prove it,' Ozzy said as he sauntered towards Boo.

'Ozzy, leave him alone,' Meg chastised, snapping her fingers.

'Spoilsport,' Ozzy muttered, returning to her side, smirking as Boo visibly relaxed.

'Please don't tell Aunt… I mean, Mrs Broom,' Meg said, looking at each of The Misfits; Ozzy's faux pas putting her in danger.

'Why would we do that?' Achoo asked.

'Well… because… well… oh, I don't know…'

'Don't worry, Meg, your secret is safe with us,' Zoe said, as she squeezed onto the swing beside the petite witch and draped her arm around her shoulders, giving her a hug.

'It's hardly a secret, since I've told you, is it?' Ozzy said, shaking his head.

'It is if she doesn't want her aunt to find out,' snapped Mina. 'So, where did you lose it?'

'Well, if she knew that, it wouldn't be lost, would it?' Ozzy snarked.

'Are you always so sarcy?' Boo stepped in.

'Moi? Sarcastic? I don't know what you mean.' Ozzy fixed his yellow glare on Boo and narrowed his eyes.

Boo glared back.

'Enough!' Meg said before bursting into fresh tears. 'I… have… to… find… it… before… school… finishes.'

'And we'll help you, won't we?' Zoe said, looking at each of her friends.

'Well, it doesn't leave us much time,' Achoo mumbled.

'Where do we even start?' asked Boo.

'Of course we will,' concluded Mina. 'I'll rephrase my earlier question and ask when you saw it last?'

'This morning.'

'When exactly?' Mina pushed.

'When she was having to prove herself to that worthless meathead.'

'Ozzy, stop it. They're trying to help.'

'If they're trying to help, they need to be looking for it then,' Ozzy sulked.

'We will once we've established the facts!' Mina snapped. 'Okay, so the last time you saw it was when you were with Jonas. What did you do with it last?'

'Put it in my backpack, like I always do. Or, at least, I thought I had.'

'Aren't you supposed to wear it?' Achoo interrupted, prompting fresh tears from Meg.

'Don't fink you're 'elping, Wolfie.'

'I was just saying.'

'Well, don't, it isn't helpful,' Mina said. 'Meg, why don't you tell us exactly what you did after your, er, altercation with Jonas?'

***

'Ummm, well, erm,' Meg mumbled as she screwed up her face, trying to remember her day. She always had trouble remembering. Auntie Gert said it was because she didn't pay enough attention, which was also the problem with her spellcasting… according to her aunt.

'Just tell them, Meg,' hissed Ozzy, his thick black tail flicking in irritation.

'I'm… trying!' Meg said out of the corner of her mouth.

'You can't remember, can you?' he said and lowered his head, raising a paw and pressing it against his eyes.

'Of course I can!'

'Then tell them!'

'Erm, well, Auntie Gert brought us to school as usual—'

'No, she didn't. We got out, remember, on the corner? You didn't want to be seen arriving with her.' Ozzie stared at Meg, his eyes wide, shaking his head.

'Oh, yes.' Meg nodded but said nothing more.

'Blimey, this in goin' to take furever,' groaned Boo.

'Shh,' snapped Zoe.

'Think I'll have a snooze,' murmured Achoo.

'How about you just tell me where you went after you put the stone back in your backpack?' Mina suggested. 'After all, you only lost it after this point, didn't you?'

'Good thinking,' Ozzy purred and sauntered over to Mina. 'Quite the clever one, aren't you?'

Mina glared over her square-framed glasses at him, and he slunk back to Meg and nudged her to respond.

'Give me a minute, I'm thinking,' she said.

Ozzy harrumphed and flopped down, his back to Meg.
'Well, I put the stone in my backpack, then—'

'If you wore it around your neck like you're supposed to, we wouldn't be here now,' grumbled Ozzy.

'It's too heavy. You know this. Why do you keep—?'

'Let's just stay focused on where you went. We don't have much time,' Mina prompted, glaring at Boo, who was about to chip in, deflating him.

'Like I said, I put the stone in my backpack, then I went to class. This was after Jonas and the others had left, you know, after my aunt came and defended me.' Meg fell silent as she looked down at the ground. She could feel tears of frustration well up and she didn't want the others to see.

'Okay, but I think you've forgotten to tell me something,' Mina said, lips pursed, her index finger tapping against them.

'No, I haven't.'

'You have, but carry on for now.'

''Ang on, Fangless, 'ow do you know she's forgot somefink?' Boo jumped in.

'Don't you know anything about vampires, Spirit Boy? I can read minds.'

'Oh really, and what am I thinkin' now then?'

'It doesn't work like that. You have to be concentrating on… oh, never mind, stop trying to distract me!' Mina turned her attention back to Meg.

'Which class did you go to first?'

'Form, then assembly, then—'

'You didn't take your backpack to assembly?'

Meg and the others stared at Mina as if she'd gone mad.

'I'm just being thorough,' she said. 'Where did you leave it?'

'Under my desk where I always do.'

'And was it still there when you got back?'

'Yes.'

'And had it been disturbed?'

''Ow on earf is she gonna know that?' scoffed Boo.

Mina fixed him with a death stare before replying, 'Because she's a girl and we know everything, don't we girls?'

'We sure do,' said Zoe.

Meg merely nodded.

'So, had someone tampered it with?' Mina asked again.

'No, I don't think so.'

'Okay, and where did you go after assembly?'

'Erm, Spellcasting for Beginners.'

'Ha ha, I bet that's a packed class, 'ey, Wolfie?' Boo guffawed and kicked a sleeping Achoo. Achoo just mumbled and turned over.

'Boo, could you maybe find something else to do as you're not helping?' Mina snapped.

'Like what?'

'Oh, I don't know, get yourself stuck in a wall or something.'

'Ouch, that's a bit below the old belt, even for you, Fangless.'

'Arghh, just be quiet then, will you!'

Boo held his hands up in mock surrender and slumped on the floor next to a now snoring Achoo.

'Finally, some peace,' Mina said, then sighed and shook her head. 'Okay, Spellcasting. That's up in the tower, isn't it?' Mina glanced at Boo from the corner of her eye, but he'd clamped his lips shut.

'Yes, at the very top. As there's only me, the school didn't want to give up a much-needed classroom.'

'So, you must have used your stone in there?'

Meg screwed up her face and looked at the sky before shaking her head. Ozzy rolled his eyes. 'Nope, it was theory today. Booorrring.'

'And then where did you go?'

'Out here, where you found me. I like to sit outside.'

'You like to avoid that worthless bully, Jonas, you mean,' said Zoe, her fists clenched as she stared towards the sports field where he was holding court.

Meg shrugged.

'So, you had no cause to get the magic stone out of your backpack all morning?' Mina asked, ignoring Zoe.

'Nope.'

'So, why did you look for it here… in the open?'

Meg shrugged. 'I always do. I like to feel it close to me.'

'Well, if you wore it, it would be—'

'Ozzy! You're not helping,' Meg scolded, before pulling him close to ease his indignation. 'I have no idea where it is. Auntie Gert is going to kill me,' Meg said, tears brimming her eyes at the thought of explaining, or not, how she'd lost the most precious thing in the world to her.

'I might,' said Mina, prompting them all to jump to attention.

'You do?' asked Meg, hope exploding in her chest and taking her breath away.

'Well, not where it is, but where you lost it,' Mina clarified.

'Oh.' Meg's shoulders slumped, and she looked at her feet.

'You know I said you'd missed something?'

'Uh-huh.'

'Well, I need you to think really hard about exactly what happened after you put the stone in your backpack.'

'I've already told—'

'No, you've skimmed over something, something

31

important. Ozzy, you can contribute if you want to.'

'Oh, thank you. Not that I need anyone's permission to—'

'Ozzy, be nice. Mina's only trying to help. They all are.'

Ozzy grumbled under his breath.

Meg looked up at the clouds and forced her mind to recount what had happened.

'Well, after Auntie Gert interrupted, I remember dropping the magic stone in my backpack. I also remember zipping it up as she was trying to get me to tell her what happened. Then I put it on my back and went to—'

'No, you didn't,' interrupted Ozzy.

'Yes, I did.'

'No, you didn't. Don't you remember? As you picked it up to put it on your back, it snagged on something?'

Meg inhaled sharply and grabbed her backpack and turned it around, inspecting it. 'Oh no!' she groaned, her fingers discovering and exploring a magic stone-sized hole in the bottom of her backpack. 'But I didn't see it, or hear it, fall out,' she wailed.

'It may well have been at the exact spot where the hole is and so you probably wouldn't have. Besides, you weren't exactly focused on your backpack, were you?'

'She's never focused on anything she's supposed to,' Ozzy interjected, earning him a stern look from Meg.

'It doesn't matter. We've established where Meg lost it. Now we need to find out where it is,' Mina said.

'Well, it's hardly going to have walked off, is it?' snarked Ozzy.

'No, but it is a stone, and stones get kicked, picked up, thrown, so it could be anywhere.'

'It's hardly just a stone,' Ozzy said. 'It's on a chain.'

Meg watched Mina's pale complexion turn puce at Ozzy's mocking tone, and she winced. She loved Ozzy to bits, but his mouth was going to get him into trouble soon.

'Be that as it may, someone may have found it and thrown it away, or anything, really. Our job is to explore all options, and not jump to conclusions.'

'Conclusions? We—'

'Zoe, Achoo!' Mina barked, startling Achoo from his slumber so quickly he wolfed out in defence.

'Yep,' Zoe said, rolling to a halt beside Mina.

'W-what's going on?' blustered Achoo as he scrabbled to his feet and tried to calm his body down. The gang snickered as parts of him turned back to a boy, while the rest remained covered in fur.

'I need you two to retrace Meg's steps from this morning, to see if you can find the stone.'

'But I've already done that,' Meg said.

'No, we've already done that,' corrected Ozzy.

'Yes, I know, but it doesn't harm to have others looking. Besides, Achoo has a keen sense of smell and should be able to pick up your scent, shouldn't you Achoo?'

'What? Oh, er, yes, retrace her steps,' he mumbled, finally getting control over his body.

'Come on then,' Zoe said. 'Break is almost over.'

***

'This is a waste of time,' Achoo grumbled, longing to be curled up behind his rock.

'Yeah, well, you know Mina, always does a thorough job,' Zoe called as she figure-eighted around him, causing the dust from the playground to swirl.

'Will you stop doing that!' Achoo said, his nose twitching as he valiantly tried to keep his sneeze at bay.

'Stop what?'

'You know what… that.' Achoo gestured towards Zoe, making a figure eight movement with his hands.

'What's the problem? I always do this. Have to keep moving. You know that.'

'I know, but you know what my allergies are like. Look what you're doing, Zoe… the dust!'

'I thought you'd got a handle on all this wolfing out business? Surely, little old me skating around you won't set you off.' Zoe laughed out loud, throwing her head back.

Achoo winced as he watched the rotting flesh of Zoe's neck stretch to breaking point.

Thank God!

He let go of the breath he'd been holding as Zoe caught the back of her head just in time. Achoo shuddered as he remembered the last time she'd done that, and hadn't caught it in time. Mrs Mort had not been happy to have to take her daughter home in pieces. Zoe had been off school for a while after that.

'Well?' Zoe prompted.

'Well, what?'

'Well, have you or haven't you got control of your wolfing out?'

Zoe changed her pattern and skated circles around Achoo instead, which did nothing to stop the dust swirling in front of him.

'I-I… achooooo!' With the first sneeze, Achoo transformed into his furry alter ego.

'Clearly not,' Zoe mumbled and grinned, increasing speed, much to Achoo's dismay.

'Zoe, please, don't, I… achoo!' And he was back again. He could already feel another sneeze building, and try as he might, Achoo couldn't stop it, nor had he had the time to focus on staying in human form, as Lew—his dad's second in command—had been teaching him. The thing was, if he had the time to prepare, he was fine, but if he didn't… well.

'Zoooooeeee, please,' he wailed, but Zoe was having too much fun, zooming around, creating different patterns, all causing the dust to hover in the air and be inhaled by Achoo, who was sneezing so fast, he was a blur of transformation.

Achoo could feel the weight of slumber rising through his body. He had to do something. With the little energy he had left, he stuck out his leg. As he intended, Zoe hit it at full speed, cartwheeling through the air, before landing in a heap in the dust.

Achoo collapsed where he stood, his leg throbbing at the force of Zoe's impact. He rubbed at his shin, his sneezing subsiding with the dust, which settled over the heap of body parts that was now Zoe.

Oh no! Panic filled Achoo's chest, squashing the exhaustion, and he crawled over to Zoe.

'I'm sorry,' he said, 'but I did ask you to stop.'

'How bad?' Zoe asked, lifting her head to survey the damage.

'Ummm, not sure, to be honest. How do I tell?'

'Well, if you lift each limb and realign me, if it stays attached, it's a thumbs up. If not, we have a job on our hands.'

'Okay, okay.' Achoo, barely able to stand himself he was so tired from the wolfing out, decided it safer to remain on all fours and straightened out Zoe's limbs. 'Good news is, both legs seem okay.'

'And my skates?'

'Your skates are fine, both still on your feet, though your dodgy ankle probably needs some attention.' Achoo untwisted Zoe's ankle to find the recently applied duct tape had come loose. He held her foot in place and re-applied the tape, but it needed to be replaced. 'Hand me your tape.'

'I don't have it with me.'

'Why not? You always carry it for emergencies such as this.'

'Didn't think I'd be needing it for a quick recon mission, did I?'

'Which we've failed at, by the way. Mina won't be happy.'

'We can still do it. She'll never know.'

'Umm, I think she might,' Achoo said, holding up Zoe's arm. 'Plus, I really don't think your ankle will hold out for much longer.'

'Oh no, not again. Mina's only just reattached it.' Zoe looked up at Achoo and smiled ruefully.

'Er, Zoe, hate to bring this to your attention, but your left eye is, er, kind of missing.'

'What? No,' Zoe cried, feeling the empty socket. 'I thought it was weird that all I could see out of it was grass.'

Achoo looked over at the lawn nearby. 'It could be anywhere, Zoe. That's a lot of grass.'

'Yeah, but you have super senses, don't you? Can't you, you know, sniff it out?'

Achoo sat and looked at Zoe, her decaying scent a permanent fixture in his nostrils. He wrinkled his nose as he pondered whether he'd be able to pick up something separate from her body.

'Hey, what are you pulling a face at? I don't smell that bad… do I?'

Achoo opened his mouth to retort, but seeing the tear brimming Zoe's eye, he swallowed back the sarcasm.

'Er, not really. I'm kind of used to it.'

'So, I do smell bad then?'

Achoo shifted uncomfortably.

Where's Boo when I need him?

'Let me see if I can find your eye. You just stay here until I get back.'

Deciding it would be quicker in wolf form, Achoo closed his eyes and screwed his face up in concentration, focusing on an image of himself as a werewolf.

'I could just make you sneeze again,' Zoe offered.

Achoo opened one eye and glared at her. 'Please don't.'

Once Zoe nodded, he closed his eye and refocused. It took a few minutes, but soon he felt the changes in his body, like a wave washing through him. When he opened his eyes again, he was on all fours.

'Won't be long,' he said and bounded off, nose to the ground.

It only took him a few minutes to locate Zoe's missing eyeball. It took him longer to change back to human form, as he kept sniggering at the thought of taking it back in his mouth. He didn't think she'd appreciate his slobber all over her eyeball, hence his decision to change back and simply carry it between his fingers.

'Here you go.' Achoo held her eyeball between his thumb and index finger, the rotting sinew dangling from the back.

'You took your time,' Zoe grumbled, snatching it off him and ramming it back into its socket. Achoo watched as she tilted her head back, careful this time, and blinked a few times. When she righted her head, the eyeball dropped forward and Achoo shot out a hand to catch it, but Zoe batted him away.

'It's fine. It always hangs out. Now, help me up. I suppose we best face the music.' Zoe gestured for Achoo to pull her up.

'What if your other arm comes off?'

'Oh, for goodness' sake, Achoo, use your head. Put your other hand on my back, so you're pushing and pulling at the same time. It's not rocket science!'

Achoo stared down at her for a moment, contemplating leaving her where she was for that comment, but he knew that's not what friends did to each other and so he sucked in his cheeks, took a breath, issued up a prayer to whoever, and did as Zoe asked, exhaling in relief when she was upright with no further lost appendages.

'I think I'll need to lean on you,' Zoe said, testing her damaged ankle and finding it wanting.

'Ummm, okay… I think.' Achoo edged up to Zoe and allowed her to drape her good arm over his shoulders, holding her loose arm in her hand.

As they made their way back to the others, the loose arm drummed its beat against Achoo's leg. He didn't like that.

***

'Where on earth have you two been? Have you seen the time?' Mina asked as she saw Zoe and Achoo approaching. 'Well, did you…' The sentence died on her lips as she saw the state they were in: Zoe carrying her severed arm… again, her ankle hanging loose; Achoo, dishevelled and clearly about to drop. 'What…happened?'

'Umm, nothing,' muttered Achoo.

'Don't lie to me,' Mina snapped.

'He's not lying,' Zoe said. 'We didn't find anything, so nothing happened, so to speak.'

'And the reason you found nothing is that something did happen, looking at the state of the pair of you!' Mina glared at them over the top of her glasses, pleased to see they had the good grace to blush. Or, she thought Zoe blushed; it was hard to tell with her green-tinged complexion. 'If we had more time, I would make you tell me, but since we don't, I won't.'

Mina raised her eyebrows as both Zoe and Achoo relaxed, Achoo settling himself down.

Probably for a sleep, Mina thought. *We'll see about that!*

'Don't even think about it. I haven't finished with you yet,' Mina said to Achoo. 'Boo, grab Zoe's backpack, will you. I need the tape.'

'Right you are, Fangless,' Boo replied, and Mina clenched her teeth together to prevent a retort. They didn't have time for more quarrels. Break would be over soon.

'But I'm tired. I just need a few minutes,' Achoo whined, as he circled, making himself comfortable.

'And you want these… Misfits helping you because?' Ozzy hissed.

Mina glared at him, but he held her stare.

'Because I think they can,' replied Meg, earning a smile from Mina.

'Achoo, I said no, I have something only you can do. Zoe, get over here so I can re-attach your arm… again,' Mina ordered.

'But my ankle…'

'Boo, help her, will you.'

'I'll try, Fangless, but you know 'ow me skills are with, 'ow shall I put this… solid objects.'

Mina closed her eyes and counted to ten. She could feel the heat rising inside her, could feel her own base instincts fighting for release. Her mother would be so pleased. She focused her mind on the task at hand and pushed the vampire back down inside. There was a time and a place, and this was neither.

'I'll help,' Meg said and raced over to Zoe, helping her up.

'You know, you could just go over to her. Wouldn't that be easier?' Ozzy yawned.

Mina glared at him again, but decided not to respond. Instead, she took Zoe's arm off her and shoved it none too gently back in its socket.

'Ouch, Mina, that hurt!'

'Well, maybe if I'd been firmer earlier, it wouldn't have come off again so soon.'

'Yeah, it would. You should have seen…' Achoo tailed off and became preoccupied with a stone.

'Right, well, we need to find some sort of lead before we have to go back to class, which gives us…' Mina stopped wrapping duct tape around Zoe's shoulder joint to glance at her watch. 'Ten minutes. Meg, do you have anything in your bag that, I don't know, may have left its scent on the stone?'

'Umm, I'm not sure,' Meg said. 'Let me have a look.'

Meg pulled her backpack forward, so it sat in the middle of the group, and then unzipped it. The four friends recoiled immediately.

'Urghhh, what on earth…?' Mina turned away in disgust.

'Wow, that smells worse than me… probably… Achoo?' Zoe commented.

'Blimey, that's a pong I never thought would assail me nostrils,' Boo said and pinched his nose.

Achoo, however, could not comment, and Mina watched, shaking her head, as he screwed his face up and shook his head, twitching his nose in the way he did when he was trying to prevent a sneeze.

This is not good.

Sure enough, Achoo lost his battle and erupted into a fit of sneezing, the results of which they'd all seen before, and so let him get on with it.

'What on earth is that smell? Garlic and…?'

'I told you it was weird,' Ozzy chipped in.

'My lunch is not weird!' Meg said, pulling her backpack against her chest.

'Well, what is it then?' asked Zoe.

'There's definitely a cheesy stink in amongst it,' said Boo.

'It's garlic, tomato and Stilton sandwiches,' Meg said.

Mina, Zoe and Boo all stared at her, before wrinkling their noses and pretending to gag.

'Well, I like them. They're my favourite,' Meg huffed.

'Well, someone has to,' Mina muttered. 'Right, well, do you think, maybe, that, er, aroma may be on your magic stone?'

Meg shrugged. 'Not sure if that's even possible.'

'Oh, believe me, Witchypoo, with a stink like that, anything is possible,' Boo guffawed.

Mina watched tears well up in Meg's eyes and pursed her lips. She walked over to Achoo, who was now lying flat on his back, legs akimbo, tongue hanging out. She visualised the little birds flying in circles around his head. 'Achoo!' She nudged him with her foot until he opened an eye.

'Hmmm,' he grunted.

'That smell… Meg's sandwiches… do you feel it's cemented in your memory?'

Achoo nodded and made to roll on his side, but Mina stopped him with her foot.

'No time to sleep. I need you to retrace Meg's steps and see if you pick up on that rather unique aroma.'

'Okay, I will, but I just need a nap first…' Achoo yawned and tried to curl up, but Mina's foot on his stomach stopped him.

'You can have a sleep after. I need you to do this now, before the bell rings and we have to go back to class.'

Achoo opened his eyes and stared up at her.

'This is important… for Meg.'

'Okay, fine,' Achoo grumbled and got to his feet. 'Where did you and Jonas face off this morning?' he asked Meg.

'O-over there.' Meg sniffed and pointed towards the school gates.

Achoo nodded and ambled off, muttering under his breath.

'You'll need to go quicker than that!' shouted Mina.

Achoo turned and stuck his tongue out before launching himself forward onto all fours.

That's more like it, Mina thought. *Wolf speed.*

***

Mina tapped her foot as she checked her watch for what seemed the thousandth time. The minute hand was moving too fast towards the end of break, and Achoo still wasn't back.

''E'll be 'avin a nap, will Wolfie,' Boo volunteered.

'How do you know?' asked Zoe, massaging her shoulder and wincing.

'Stop messing with your arm or it'll come loose again,' Mina scolded.

'Well, you've kind of put it back a bit too tight,' grumbled Zoe.

'Maybe it'll stay in place for a while then,' retorted Mina.

'Do you think he'll have gone for a nap… really?' asked Meg, her small voice making Mina reach out and squeeze her shoulder.

'No, he knows how important this is. He'll stay awake.'

I hope.

'We'll see,' said Ozzy, as he stretched before settling down close to Meg.

'Well, wonders never cease, 'ere's Wolfie now.'

They all looked up to see Achoo, in wolf form, loping towards them. He stopped a few feet away, screwed his face up, and slowly morphed back into a boy. Mina, Zoe, Boo and Meg all looked away, cringing. Only Ozzy watched with interest.

'That looks really painful,' Zoe commented when Achoo was back to himself.

'You get used to it,' he said, shrugging. 'Has the bell gone yet?'

'I fink you might of 'eard it, if it 'ad, Wolfie, what wiv your super senses.'

Achoo glared at Boo.

'Well?' Mina prompted.

'Well, what?'

'Oh, for goodness' sake, Achoo! Did you find anything?'

'Nope, not a trace.'

'Nooooooo!' wailed Meg, making them all jump.

'It's okay,' Mina said, just as the bell rang to mark the end of break. 'We will find your magic stone. I promise.'

She gave Meg a hug before they all trooped to chemistry. Mr Shelley was a stickler for punctuality.

An Unusual Whiff in Chemistry

'Well, well, you're all late,' Mr Shelley announced as Achoo, Mina, Meg, Boo and Zoe trooped into class.

''Ardly,' retorted Boo as he took his seat at the back.

Meg took the desk next to him, her backpack clutched against her chest. Ozzy jumped on her desk to observe.

Zoe took the last remaining desk in the back row and no sooner had she sat down than her feet were in motion—though she did remember to favour her damaged ankle—her blades rolling back and forth, faster and faster.

Achoo flopped into the nearest chair and promptly slid as far down as he could and closed his eyes. Within seconds, his mouth was drooping open as his chest rose and fell rhythmically.

Boo, not one to waste an opportunity, tore a sheet of paper from his exercise book and ripped it up, rolling the remnants into tiny balls. He flicked the balls at Achoo's mouth, the rest of the class giggling as Achoo waved his hand at them as though swatting flies.

Mr Shelley, after his initial rebuke, had turned his back on the class and was busy setting up an experiment.

Mina watched him curiously as she made her way to her usual window seat. There she could stare outside and watch the birds and butterflies while still half listening to her lessons. She liked Mr Shelley, as did most of the class. He wasn't like the other teachers. Yes, he made an issue if they were late, but he soon forgot it as he absorbed himself in the task he would set his class. Mr Shelley liked to have fun. Every class, he had them combining various chemicals and elements to see what the effect would be before they settled down to the task of learning about chemistry.

With his wild blue hair, greenish tinged skin—although not as green as Zoe's—moth-eaten suits, clumpy boots and wild eyes, Mr Shelley had all the makings of a mad scientist, Mina's mother often commented, but without a laboratory. She would always add, "thank goodness", and Mina would snigger. Mr Shelley's pre-class experiments were a closely guarded secret, known only to Mr Shelley and his students.

Mina watched as Mr Shelley scooped some white powder into a beaker and added some sugar, before using a pipette to drop a small amount of liquid onto the powder. Within seconds, the combination erupted into a violet flame, billowing smoke, which raced for the ceiling.

'Whoa!' commented the entire class, their attention no longer on Boo and Achoo, but where it was intended… at the front of the class.

'So, that's today's little experiment, which, as usual, you will all be allowed to practise before… And what time do you call this?' Mr Shelley frowned at the back of the class, and Mina turned to see the ever-tardy Jonas and Griff barging into the classroom.

They mumbled incoherently as they shoved through the desks, jostling Achoo to get to the last remaining empty desks… at the front.

'Ah, good, exactly where I can keep an eye on you. Now, perhaps you two can tell me what I added to the potassium chlorate and sugar to make it burn the stunning violet colour?' Mr Shelley raised his eyebrows as he stared at the two latecomers, both of whom had become fascinated with their chemistry text books.

That's a first, Mina thought as she shot her hand up in the air and bounced up and down in her seat.

'Yes, yes, Mina, I know *you* know, but what about everyone else, hey?' Mr Shelley glanced around the class. Mina followed his gaze to see everyone finding something else to do other than engage with him. Finally, both their gazes rested on Achoo.

Oh no.

Mina could see his face getting redder and redder as he tried to hold in the sneeze that was about to explode.

'Achoo, are you all right?' Mr Shelley asked, and began to approach, but Achoo shook his head and gestured for Mr Shelley to stay back.

Mina winced as Achoo lost out to his senses and began sneezing uncontrollably, wolfing in and out as he did so.

The entire class erupted in laughter, everyone that was except Mina, Boo, Zoe and Meg. They all knew what effect this had on Achoo.

'Achoo, for goodness' sake, get a grip, will you,' Mr Shelley said, staring down at Achoo, who was at the mercy of his sneezing.

'I-I c-can't,' he managed.

'How long is this going to go on for?' Mr Shelley asked, looking pointedly at Mina.

'Who knows? It depends what set him off. I think it best he leaves the room so he can calm down. Don't you agree, Mr Shelley?'

Mr Shelley looked at Mina for a few seconds, all the while Achoo was sneezing, before he nodded.

'Very well. Take him to the infirmary, but make sure

you come straight back. I don't want to have to explain to your mother why you missed the class.' Mr Shelley shuddered, and Mina swore she saw his skin turn grey for a moment before he shook it off. 'Well, what are you waiting for? You'll just have to miss the experiment, but I'm sure you can replicate it to perfection.'

Mina could. She loved the whoosh as the sulphuric acid reacted with the potassium chlorate, and the subsequent violet flame was mesmerising. Of course, her mother went mad, as the smoke tended to infiltrate the upper hallways, saying it played havoc with her complexion, not to mention Mina's.

Sighing, Mina pushed away from her desk and dragged Achoo out of class, his body still transforming with his sneezes, despite the fact he'd somehow fallen asleep.

***

'There's a surprise, Wolfie's asleep,' Boo said as the friends trooped into the infirmary to see Achoo.

'It was kind of excessive, even for him, don't you think?' Zoe said, taking advantage of the space and the tiled floor, zooming in and out of everyone, narrowly missing the nurse who was checking on Achoo.

'Do you want to end up in here too?' the nurse admonished, but Zoe just shrugged and smiled. The nurse left, shaking her head and muttering.

'Achoo, it's us,' Mina called as she rocked Achoo to rouse him.

'Mmmmmm,' Achoo replied.

'Achoo, wake up,' Mina urged, but again Achoo merely mumbled and curled up in a tighter ball.

'Allow me,' Boo interjected and, bending down so his mouth was next to Achoo's ear, he bellowed, 'Wake up, Wolfie!'

Zoe, Meg and Mina all jumped at the sudden noise. Achoo, however, swatted Boo out of the way and rolled over.

'Oh, for goodness' sake, have they given him something to help him sleep?' Mina asked.

'Don't fink Wolfie needs any 'elp in that department,' Boo said, leaning against the wall and observing a slumbering Achoo.

'I know what might work,' Meg offered.

Mina, Boo and Zoe turned to look at her, eyebrows raised.

Meg held up her backpack. 'Perhaps a whiff of this?'

'That ought to do it,' concurred Ozzy.

'For once, I agree with the fleabag,' Boo said, crossing his arms and nodding.

'I am not a fleabag!' Ozzy hissed before stalking off, tail in the air, and sitting by the door.

'Well, go on then,' Zoe urged.

As Meg approached Achoo, unzipping her backpack as she went, the others drew back, not wanting to be in the firing line.

Meg held the backpack open and wafted it in front of Achoo's slumbering face.

Almost immediately, his nose twitched, then his mouth, and then his hand came up to swat away the irritation. Meg retreated a few steps until he'd settled before coming forward again and holding the open backpack even closer. Once again, the twitching started, but this time no amount of swatting could get rid of the irritation. They all watched as Achoo gulped in huge lungfuls of air before erupting into a fit of coughing that not only woke him up, but sent him crashing to the floor.

'I think that's enough now, Meg,' Mina said, indicating for Meg to close her backpack.

While the friends waited for Achoo to calm down, they went about their business: Boo hovered cross-legged in the air whilst trying to pick up the chart from the end of Achoo's bed; Zoe skated in figure-eights, making them larger, then smaller, her speed never slowing; Meg went over to placate a sulking Ozzy; and Mina stood in front of Achoo, arms crossed, foot tapping, lips pursed.

'Have you finished?' she asked when Achoo's sneezing finally stopped and he flopped back against the side of the bed.

'I-I think so,' he murmured, closing his eyes.

'Don't even think about going back to sleep,' Mina said, grabbing his shirt and hauling him to his feet.

Achoo flopped back on the bed, but a swift kick from Mina to his dangling shin soon had him sitting bolt upright.

'Hey guys,' he said, grinning at them all, his eyes half-closed.

'Never mind that,' Mina said. 'What on earth set you off in class?'

'Er, well, the same stink that set me off just now. What else?'

'But how? Meg came in with us and sat at the back. You were fine then—'

'Until Jonas and Griff came in,' Zoe interrupted Mina, stopping so quickly she barrelled through a still hovering Boo and straight into Mina, who prevented them both from falling.

'That's right,' Mina said. 'They were late and—'

'They clumped right past Wolfie and then he 'ad his melodramatic sneezing fit,' Boo interrupted.

'Why do you all keep interrupting me?' Mina demanded.

'Because, lovely as you are, Fangless, you take too long and we ain't got all day.'

Mina opened her mouth to retort, but decided he wasn't worth the effort. Instead, she gave him one of her best glares, over the rim of her glasses. Boo smiled sweetly at her and blew her a kiss, making Mina growl.

'Does this mean Jonas and Griff have my magic stone?' Meg piped up from near the door.

Tearing her glare away from a simpering Boo, Mina turned to Meg. 'It certainly seems that way.'

'Great, thanks, guys.' Meg turned to leave, Ozzy pinned to her side.

'Hang on a minute, Meg. Where are you going?' Zoe asked, rolling to the doorway to block Meg's exit.

'To ask them for my stone back.'

Achoo, Mina, Zoe and Boo looked at each other before looking back at Meg and bursting out laughing.

'Stop it, guys,' Mina hissed as she saw tears welling up in Meg's eyes. She waited for them to quieten down before she spoke again. 'Meg, there is absolutely no way that Jonas or Griff, or whoever has your magic stone, will just give it you back.'

'Why not? It doesn't belong to them.'

'No, it doesn't, but they still won't give it back.'

'But why?'

'Because they don't like you, do they?' Boo said, floating over to lean against the wall beside Meg.

'But what's that got to do with it?' Meg asked, frowning. Ozzy sat beside her, his tail swishing to reflect her irritation.

'I hate to say this, Meg, but it has everything to do with it,' Zoe added.

Meg looked from one to the other, her bottom lip trembling, tears still threatening.

'Jonas and Griff are bullies,' Mina said, putting her arm

around Meg's shoulders. 'Well, Jonas is the bully, Griff is… well…'

'His sidekick,' Zoe volunteered.

'Not what I was looking for, but probably more polite,' Mina acknowledged. 'Bullies don't return things when they can use it to torture you with instead.'

'But they *have* to give it back,' Meg said.

'But they won't,' Mina said again.

'But they have to,' insisted Meg.

'Why?' asked Zoe.

'Because it's 'ers, Skater Girl.'

'No… well… yes… but because it's dangerous when it's away from me.'

'Dangerous how?' Mina asked, her hackles rising.

'If the stone's away from me, it has nowhere for its power to go.'

'So?' Boo said, shrugging.

'So, the power builds up inside the stone until…' Meg tailed off and picked Ozzy up, holding him close to her as she shuddered.

'Meg, what happens to the stone if the power builds up?' Mina asked, clicking her fingers in front of Meg's face to get her attention.

'It explodes,' Meg said, before running from the room, leaving Mina, Zoe and Boo staring after her, mouths agape.

Achoo's mouth was also agape, but that was because he was snoring soundly.

Tackling the Bullies

Hidden from view and with Ozzy grasped against her so he couldn't give them away, Meg stood spying on Jonas and Griff as they rough and tumbled in the privacy of their yard. They classed it as their yard because no one else dared enter unless given permission. It just wasn't worth it.

Well, Jonas is doing the roughing, she thought as he cuffed Griff around the ear again, knocking the faithful servant to the ground. *Boys!*

'Well, are you going? I'm kind of suffocating here,' Ozzy hissed as he dug his claws into Meg's chest.

She let out a yelp and then froze, anxious Jonas might have heard, but as she peered around the corner of the building, she could see that wasn't the case. Jonas now had Griff in a headlock, Griff's face an unworldly shade of purple.

'Why, oh why, does that idiot worship him so much?' Ozzy muttered, shaking his head as Meg released her hold on him. He landed on all four paws and proceeded to clean himself.

'I haven't got germs, you know,' Meg said, crossing her arms and staring down at Ozzy, who shrugged and carried on.

Meg looked back at the boys. 'He puts up with it because people know who he is when he's with Jonas.'

'It's hardly worth it, is it?' Ozzy yawned, grooming done.

'It is if you're nobody,' Meg said, then sighed and looked at her feet.

'You're not nobody, Meg, you're somebody.' Ozzy rubbed himself around Meg's legs, purring.

'Not without my magic stone, I'm not.'

'Well, go and get it back.'

Meg didn't reply. Instead, she took deep breaths, clenching and unclenching her hands, her palms sweaty.

I can do this. I can do this.

'Okay,' she announced a moment later and strode forward.

***

'Who gave you permission to come here?' Griff demanded, bodyguard mode enabled as he made himself as wide as he could, putting himself between Meg and Jonas as he stared at her.

It amused Meg to see Griff do this because, number one, Jonas didn't need a bodyguard—he was big enough and powerful enough to stand up for himself; and number two, Griff wasn't that much taller than her, but he was wide. In fact, Griff was so wide, he could hide many things from view, if only he were taller. Sadly, though, his legs hadn't grown in proportion to his body, but his arms had, almost touching the floor and earning him the nickname of Gorilla. Not to his face, obviously. Meg looked at his face now, with his lower jaw protruding forward of his top one and his sparsely decorated head, and felt it was an insult to gorillas everywhere. Still, Coach Banks found him an asset in the sports arena for reasons she could never fathom.

'I'm talking to you, witch. What you doing here? No one invited you.'

Meg stopped and stared Griff in the eyes. 'I've come to get my magic stone back.'

'Magic stone? What magic stone? We have no clue what you're talking about, do we, Jonas?' Griff said, spreading his long arms wide and turning the corners of his mouth down, making him look like a sea bass rather than a gorilla.

'Oh, I don't know,' Jonas said, sidling over and leaning his arm on Griff's head as he fixed Meg with his most dazzling—and supposedly disarming—smile, his fangs glistening. 'Are you looking for this?'

Meg saw Griff deflate at Jonas's admission, before she turned her attention to the stone on display between Jonas's thumb and forefinger.

'That's the one,' she said, and jumped as high as she could, trying to grab the stone. Jonas simply lifted his arm, holding it way beyond her reach.

'Not so fast, Witchypoo. You can't want it that much if you threw it away.'

'I didn't throw it away, Jonas,' Meg said, teeth gritted, fists clenched. 'I lost it.'

'That's even worse. If it was that valuable to you, you'd never let it out of your sight now, would you?'

Jonas bent in half so he could look Meg in the eyes.

With every ounce of her being, she wanted to wipe the self-satisfied smirk off his oh so handsome face, but she needed the magic stone for that.

'That's what I always tell her,' chipped in Ozzy, 'But does she listen to me?'

'Not helping, Ozzy,' Meg hissed.

'What's the fur ball whining about now?' Jonas said, sneering as he looked down his nose at Ozzy.

'I didn't lose it on purpose,' Meg said, ignoring Jonas's question.

'Well, of course, no one loses things on purpose, but you did… you know… lose it, so it can't be that valuable to you.' Jonas threw the stone up in the air and Meg thought her heart would stop as she held her breath, praying he would catch it, praying he wouldn't let it fall to the ground. But as the stone dropped out of the glare of the sun, a far more catastrophic worry lodged itself in Meg's chest.

The magic stone had turned from its milky-lilac resting state to an ominous shade of violet.

'That's not good,' she muttered.

'What isn't?' Ozzy asked.

'The stone, look at it.' Meg tilted her head toward the falling stone and Ozzy looked up, his eyes growing wide as the seriousness of the situation registered.

'We have to get that stone back,' he said.

'You think?'

'Okay, enough,' snapped Jonas, snatching the stone from the air. 'What are you and the powder puff talking about? Because I know you're talking to it.'

Ozzy growled, and Meg rested her hand on his head to calm him.

'You need to give me my stone back. It's dangerous if you don't.'

'What? This?' Jonas said, holding the stone up again. Meg glanced at it to see it pulsating between his fingers.

'Yes, can't you see? The colour, the pulsing, it shouldn't be doing that.'

'What are you talking about? It's not *doing* anything. It's just a stone, like any other.'

'But it isn't just a stone, Jonas, it's my magic stone. You know that.'

'Do I? Do we, Griff? Do we know it's her magic stone?'

'Nah, Jonas, it's just a pretty stone we found on the ground, that's all,' Griff said, glowing at being brought into the debate.

'Please, Jonas, I need it back.'

Jonas looked down his nose at Meg and pursed his lips, rubbing his chin with his free hand, his foot tapping. 'What do you think, Griff? Shall we give her stone back?'

'Erm, well, erm…' Griff's eyes flitted left and right as he fidgeted, clearly not used to being asked for his opinion. 'I think it's up to you, Jonas.'

'Good answer, my friend. Good answer. And I think that, if the witch tells us why she needs this stone so badly, then I'll give it back to her. So, what's it to be, Broom?'

'Meg, don't,' hissed Ozzy. 'You know the rules.'

'I know, but I need to get the stone back.'

'Not like this, you don't. Besides, you know he won't give it back even if you do tell him… don't you?'

Meg looked into Ozzy's eyes. She knew he was right. The magic stone and its powers were a secret known only to the witches, a secret that should not be shared with outsiders.

She sighed. 'Look, I didn't want to have to do this, but if you don't, I'm going to have to tell the headmaster.'

'You can't do that. Have you never heard of "finders keepers, losers weepers"?' asked Jonas, sneering.

'You leave me no other choice,' Meg said.

'Well, you do have one other choice,' Ozzy hissed, prowling up and down in front of Meg. 'I could just rip his—'

'No!' Meg shouted, making them all jump.

'No what, Witchypoo? I haven't said anything,' Jonas said. 'Not talking to the puffball again, are you?'

'Jonas, if she tells Count Orloff, your uncle, you—'

'I know he's my uncle, stupid,' snapped Jonas.

'Well, you know what he'll do…'

'She won't tell him, will you, Broom?'

'Yes, I-I will.'

'No, you won't.'

'Yes, I will.'

'Er, no, you won't.'

'Dear Satan, this could go on for hours,' Ozzy said.

'Why don't you think I'll tell him?'

'Well, because if you do, then I'll just tell Mrs Broom that you lost your precious stone.'

Meg stared up into the smug smile plastered on Jonas's face.

If he tells Auntie Gert... Meg felt tears brim her eyes and she fought to keep them at bay, but it was too late.

'Oh dear, looks like we've won, Griff. Someone can't admit she's lost the stone, can she?'

Meg didn't answer, not trusting her voice or her emotions.

'Let me at him,' Ozzy hissed, but Meg had hold of him by the scruff of the neck.

'Come on, let's leave this cry baby to her misery,' Jonas said, elbowing Griff and sending him six feet across the yard.

Griff soon picked himself up and loped after Jonas, who strode out of sight, tossing the stone up in the air and catching it as he did so.

'Oh, Ozzy, what am I going to do?'

The Runial Retrieval Plan

'I'll catch up with you in a minute,' Zoe called back, skidding to a halt outside the girls' toilets. She looked at the others, miles behind her as always, including Achoo, who'd just been released from the infirmary.

Did they hear me?

Zoe shrugged. It didn't matter if they did. There was every chance she'd be out before they even caught up. She pushed the door open and rolled into the room, humming to herself as she wove this way and that.

It took a few moments for her to register the other noise in the room. Zoe stopped everything she was doing and listened. Sure enough, from behind the only closed cubicle door came the definite sound of weeping.

'Hello?' Zoe said. 'Who's in there? Are you okay?'

The weeping stopped, to be replaced with a loud sniff, followed by a hiccup. But no reply came.

Unperturbed, Zoe got down on her knees and peered under the door. There sat Meg, her knees pulled in tightly, her forehead resting on top of them.

'Meg? What's wrong? Why are you crying?'

Meg looked up, resting her chin on her knees, and Zoe saw her fighting back the tears and her bottom lip wobbling.

'Talk to me, Meg. What happened?'

'J-Jonas.'

Zoe clenched her teeth and heard her jaw dislocate,

catching it in time and clicking it back into place. She opened and closed her mouth a few times to make sure all was well before she spoke. 'What did he do?'

'H-he w-wouldn't g-give me back m-my stone.' Meg sniffed again and wiped away fresh tears with her fist.

'So he has it, then?' Zoe shifted position as the sinews in her limbs lengthened a little too much.

Meg nodded.

'Look, Meg, sorry about this, but can you come out? It's getting a bit difficult for me to keep it together down here.'

But Meg shook her head and burst into fresh tears.

'Okay then, but I'm going to have to come in, and you'll have to help me when I do.'

Meg frowned, but Zoe gave no further explanation. Instead, she detached the limbs she knew wouldn't survive the scuffle and shoved them under the door, before dragging the rest of herself inside the cubicle, nudging Meg over so she could rest against the toilet.

'Right, can you get the duct tape out of my backpack and help me put these back?' Zoe held her wayward arm and foot. 'And whilst you're doing it, you can tell me what happened. Sound good?'

Meg stared wide-eyed at Zoe and nodded, before rummaging in Zoe's backpack for the vital roll of duct tape.

***

'Of course we're going to help you,' Mina announced. 'Aren't we?' She glared at Boo and Achoo, who had distanced themselves from a still sobbing Meg, and a rather badly put back together Zoe.

'Well?' she demanded as she adjusted Zoe's duct tape.

'Hey, be gentle,' Zoe grumbled as Mina yanked the duct tape higher, securing her arm at the same level as the other.

'Well, stop falling apart! Boo! Achoo! Pay attention.

Meg needs our help, and I feel we can—and should—all play our parts in doing that.'

'An' what did you 'ave in mind, Fangless?'

Mina narrowed her eyes at Boo, but resisted the urge to quarrel with him over the nickname she hated. Instead, she rolled her shoulders back and said, 'I have a plan. Let's find an empty room and I'll share it with you all.'

Mina marched off down the corridor, Zoe and Meg behind her. Boo, on the other hand, was left with the job of rousing Achoo from forty winks before they could follow.

***

'So, do you all know what you're doing?' Mina asked.

No one responded.

'Well?'

Still, no one replied.

'Achoo? What do you need to do?'

'Erm, find Jonas and Griff?' Achoo said, looking around the group.

'But I know where they are,' Meg said. 'I've just left them.'

'Yes, but they may have moved on and Achoo is best equipped to track them down,' Mina said. 'Are you clear on what you need to do?'

'Get Jonas to show me my magic stone again,' Meg said.

'Correct.'

'But what if he won't?'

'He will. Don't you worry about that. He can't help but brag about what he's got,' Zoe said and snorted.

'Once Jonas has shown us the stone, Boo and I will distract him and Griff and—'

''Ow are we gonna do that, Fangless?'

'Honestly, Boo, don't you listen to anything I say?' Mina rolled her eyes in exasperation before glaring at Boo.

'I will change into an animal they don't like… I'm thinking a snake—'

'But 'ow do you know they don't like snakes?'

'I just do,' said Mina, winking at Zoe. Zoe giggled.

'Oh, I've so got to 'ear this story,' Boo said, crossing his arms as he levitated cross-legged.

'Not today you haven't,' Mina said. 'Today, you'll be invisible to help me distract them, remember? You're with Griff. I'm with Jonas.'

'Right you are, Fangless.'

'And Zoe, you—'

'I know, I know. I'll swipe the stone and skate away at top speed,' Zoe said.

'And we'll meet back here. I know it's lunchtime and we have plenty of time, but the sooner we get it done, the better. Agreed?'

Mumbles of agreement followed.

'Great! Achoo? It's over to you,' Mina said.

'Er, well, er, shall we just head to Jonas's yard?' Achoo looked from one to the other, his arms spread wide, shrugging.

'Oh, Satan in hell,' Ozzy said, looking down at the ground.

'Achoo, we need you to use that sense of smell of yours to sniff out their location… and the stone,' Mina urged.

'I can give you another sniff, if you like?' Meg offered, unzipping her backpack.

'Oh no, no, no, no. That's a whiff I won't forget in a long time,' Achoo said, recoiling. 'Give me a minute.'

They stood back and watched as Achoo screwed his face up in concentration.

'Not gonna say what Wolfie looks like he's doing,' Boo whispered, nudging Zoe.

'Shh! He needs to focus,' Mina hissed.

After a minute, they all winced and turned away, except Ozzy, as Achoo morphed into his alter ego and bounded off.

'Wait for us, Achoo!' yelled Mina as they all hurried after him.

Reunited

'Good job you was a sniffin', ain't it, Wolfie?' Boo leaned against the side of the sports hall, his arms crossed.

Achoo, still in wolf form, glared at him before fixing his gaze on the two people he'd tracked as they trooped across the sports field towards one of the benches scattered around for spectators. 'It wasn't exactly difficult to know where they'd be if not in their yard.'

'Still, credit where credit's due, hey, Fangless?'

Mina frowned at Boo. 'Not yet, Achoo. We might need you to sniff out the stone.'

'But I thought Meg's job was to get them to show the stone?' Achoo fidgeted, closing his eyes and gritting his teeth.

'He's at it again!' Boo quipped.

'You have no idea how hard it is to stay like this, do you?' Achoo snapped.

'Aw, come on, Wolfie, don't tell me you is still in trainin' like Meg 'ere.' Boo didn't even flinch as Achoo launched himself at him, ramming straight into the wall, as Boo knew he would. He transformed back in an instant, his concentration instead on massaging the top of his head to minimise the bump.

'Great, thanks Boo,' Mina said, shaking her head at Achoo who had sprawled out on the floor. 'Right, Meg, you're up.'

'What? You're not coming with me?' Meg's eyes were

like saucers as she stared at Mina.

'He's more likely to show you the magic stone if you're alone,' she said, smiling what she hoped was an encouraging smile.

'Don't want to be a party pooper, but isn't it stealing if we take it from Jonas?' Zoe asked as she skated around, making patterns on the dusty tarmac.

'No, because it doesn't belong to Jonas and Griff. All we're doing is finding it and returning it to its rightful owner, who in this case is Meg,' Mina said.

'But Jonas said something about finders keepers—'

'Losers weepers,' finished Boo.

'As I was saying,' Meg said, frowning at Boo, 'Jonas said "finders keepers, losers weepers" when I asked for the stone back, so does that mean it *is* his… because he found it?'

'Not necessarily. If you find something, you should always try to track down the rightful owner, as the person could be in dire need of what they've lost, and be devastated,' Mina said with authority.

'Like me.'

'Yes, like you, Meg. And the fact Jonas knows you've lost it and you need it makes what he's doing a lot worse.'

'But what if you can't find the owner?' Achoo asked, pushing himself up to sitting.

'Well, if you can't find the owner and they don't come forward to claim it, then you can keep it,' Mina continued.

'But 'ow long does you 'ave to wait before you can keep it?' Boo rubbed his chin as he pondered.

'It would depend on whether you've had to advertise, I suppose. You need to give people time to see the advert and respond.' Mina nodded to herself, satisfied with her explanation.

'So, Jonas has to give me it back.'

'Yes, of course he does,' Mina said and patted Meg's shoulder.

Ozzy had been observing the conversation through slitted eyes as he studied the two people horsing around on the sports field. 'Can we get this over with?' he said. 'I'm bored.'

***

'Are you following us, Broom?' Griff, once again, placed himself in front of Jonas as Meg approached them across the sports field, Ozzy by her side.

'And you brought the furball. How nice,' Jonas added as he looked down his nose at Ozzy and sneered, his top lip curling back to reveal his fangs.

'Two can play at that game,' muttered Ozzy, doubling the size of his body as all his fur stood on end and he hissed at Jonas, showing all of his teeth.

'Hush, Ozzy, you're not helping,' Meg said, placing a calming hand on his head. He deflated in an instant and instead glared up at Jonas.

'Not helping with what, witch?' Jonas asked.

'I want my stone back.'

'Not this again,' Griff yawned. 'Are you deaf, Broom? Jonas said finders keepers, which means it's his.'

'But it isn't his, is it?'

'Ey?' Griff scrunched up his face and scratched his head, turning to Jonas for support.

'What our young witch here means is that it isn't "finders keepers" because I know who the stone belongs to. Isn't that right, Broom?'

'Yes, so you need to return it to me.'

Jonas and Griff looked at each other before bursting out laughing. Griff fell over and rolled around on the floor.

'What's so funny?' Meg asked, fighting back the tears that were threatening.

'Oh, I don't know, Broom, maybe the fact you actually think I'm going to give *this* back to you.'

Meg and Ozzy gasped as Jonas pulled the magic stone from his pocket, the angry violet throbbing inside the stone.

'B-but Jonas, the stone, look at it. Can't you feel it?'

'Feel what, Broom? It's just a stone. It's no different from earlier.'

'But it is, it's—'

'Arghh, what was that?' Griff yelped and pushed over onto his hands and knees, turning this way and that, yelping every so often.

'What was what?' Jonas asked, sighing and rolling his eyes as he turned to Griff.

Meg glanced back towards the sports hall to see Achoo giving her the thumbs up as Zoe readied herself for launch.

'Can't you see it? There's something there. It keeps touching me. Arghh!'

'Pull yourself together, you're making a fool out of yourself, and me,' Jonas snapped.

'Meg! Look,' hissed Ozzy, nodding towards Jonas's feet.

Meg dragged her gaze from a writhing Griff to see a snake, the colour of the sports field, nudging itself under the hem of Jonas's trouser leg. She clamped a hand over her mouth to suppress a giggle.

'Jonas, help me!' screamed Griff as he suddenly arched backwards.

'Oh, for Satan's sake, get a grip!' Jonas said and as he leaned forward to drag Griff to his feet. Mina, in snake form, slithered up Jonas's trouser leg.

'Arghh! Get it out! Get it out!' Jonas yelled, clawing at his leg.

For a moment, Meg lost sight of the magic stone, but when she saw Jonas's fist glowing, she knew it was there. She turned to check on Zoe's progress and spun around in a circle as Zoe zoomed past her and barrelled into Jonas. The impact loosened his grip, and Zoe swiped the stone.

Meg gasped as Zoe's arm dropped because of the impact and she rushed forward to catch it, but Zoe was too quick, grasping it and the stone close as she headed back towards the sports hall.

Moments later, the snake reappeared and slithered away, and then Meg felt herself propelled backwards. Ozzy had to exert himself to catch up.

***

'Blimey, that was close, Skater Girl,' Boo said as he collapsed, out of breath at having concentrated for so long.

'What choice did I have? I could see his fist glowing, and I couldn't think of any other way to get him to release it. Ouch!' Zoe grumbled as Mina, for what seemed the thousandth time that day, secured Zoe's wayward arm.

'Your mother is going to go spare when she sees the state of you,' Mina commented.

'Nah, she's used to it,' Zoe said, and winked. 'It's no worse than normal… not really.'

'Is it all right… the stone?' Achoo asked. He hadn't been able to tear his gaze away from it since Zoe brought it back. It looked angrier than his dad did when he found him asleep.

'Not really,' Meg said, pressing her hand against the glowing stone as it hung from the chain around her neck.

'Well, if you'd only had it there all along,' Ozzy muttered.

'Yes, Ozzy, you've made your point. It's there now,' Meg said.

'What's wrong with it?' Achoo asked, his gaze glued to the stone.

'Oi, Wolfie, it's rude to stare, especially like that at girls,' Boo commented, doubling over in laughter as Achoo's cheeks reddened.

Achoo dragged his gaze away from the stone. 'I'm so sorry,' he said, 'But, why is it like that... you know... throbbing?'

'You can see that?' Meg asked. 'All of you?'

The Misfits nodded.

'That's strange. Jonas didn't see it,' she continued.

'Maybe the stone didn't want him to?' Achoo suggested.

The others looked at him quizzically, and Achoo felt himself blush again and shrugged. 'Whatever.'

'Maybe you're right,' Meg said, holding the stone. 'I thought only witches could see its power, but maybe the stone chooses who sees it.'

'Yes, yes, this is all very nice, but if you don't do something about the stone soon, you know what will happen, and then what?' Ozzy said.

'What will happen?' asked Achoo, beating the others to it.

Meg looked at Ozzy, who shrugged.

'I shouldn't really tell you, but I guess it's okay as, without you guys, I wouldn't have got my magic stone back.' Meg looked at Ozzy again, and this time he nodded. 'Umm, the magic stone isn't supposed to be separated from me. When it is, which it never has been before, nor will it ever be again, the power of the stone has nowhere to go, because I'm not there to absorb it.'

'What happens?' Achoo asked.

'Give 'er a chance to tell you, Wolfie.' Boo shook his

head as Mina and Zoe remained silent, waiting for Meg to finish.

'Well, the power builds up, and the stone turns dark violet, the power inside fighting to get out. Look… have a feel.' Meg removed the stone from around her neck and handed it to Mina, who jolted back at the force of the stone before handing it to Zoe.

'So, what do you have to do?' Mina asked as Boo and Achoo squabbled over who should hold the stone after Zoe.

'Erm, well, I need to release it before it gets to the point when the stone explodes.'

'What? Really?' Zoe said, her eyes wide.

'What 'appens if it explodes?' asked Boo, leaning forward with interest as he studied the stone more closely.

Meg pulled it out of his hand and secured it back around her neck. 'If it explodes, it will do a lot of damage… and harm.'

'So, what do you need to do to release the power, then?' Mina asked.

'Spells. It's as simple as that. But I need somewhere out of the way to do it, as I don't really want the entire school seeing.'

'Wouldn't they leave you alone if they did?' Zoe piped up.

'Yes, but my aunt… Mrs Broom, would know what had happened.'

''Ow?'

'Because of the sort of spells I need to do.'

'We could do it in the woods, where the pack meets,' Achoo suggested. 'It's away from school and no one really goes there.'

'But when? It sounds quite urgent,' Mina said.

'As long as it's today, I'll be okay. And it needs to be

before school finishes as my… Mrs Broom gives me a lift home.'

'You don't 'ave to keep callin' her Mrs B. We know she's your aunt.'

Meg shrugged.

'We could go during afternoon break. We have a free period after, so no one would really miss us,' Zoe suggested.

'Well, they would if they saw us all trooping out together,' Mina said, tapping her chin with her forefinger. 'I think if we all leave separately and meet on the corner, we should be okay. We must make sure we're back before school finishes, though, so we can leave with everyone else.'

'Agreed,' they all said at once.

Heroes!

'Look at him,' Zoe laughed, nudging Mina.

Mina, who was enjoying the afternoon sun warming her face, opened her eyes and looked to where Zoe nodded. 'Well, he has had a feed now, so if anything will send him to sleep, that will.'

'True enough,' Zoe said. 'But what's Boo's excuse?'

Mina smiled as she saw Boo sitting against a tree trunk, his arms crossed and his head bowed. 'Oh, I don't think he's asleep, are you, Boo?'

'Nothin' gets past you, does it, Fangless?' Boo said, lifting his head and grinning, before stretching and letting out an enormous belch. ''Scuse me, no offence meant,' he said, covering his mouth.

'Loads taken,' Zoe retorted. 'How did she do it, do you think?'

'Do what?' Mina asked as she too looked at Meg, who was consulting with Ozzy not far away.

'Get that food to just follow us as we walked. It was like the Pied Piper. No one even noticed.'

'I know, weird, hey,' Mina said, pursing her lips. 'Hey, Meg?'

'What's up?' Meg asked as she wandered over, Ozzy close by.

'Zoe and I want to know how you got that food to follow us here. We didn't see or hear you do any spells, plus no one batted an eye.'

'To be honest, I'm not sure. I was just talking to Ozzy about it. All I can say is I was thinking about the plan, you know, of what I wanted to do for you guys, and by the time we got here, most of it had followed.'

'FIC,' Ozzy said. 'At last.'

'What's FIC?' Zoe and Mina asked at the same time.

'I knows this,' Boo said, sauntering over to join the conversation. 'Focus, intent and concentration.'

'How do you know that?' Meg asked.

'You'd be surprised what I can find out, bein' in the lack of state that I is.'

'But what does it mean?' Mina asked.

'Let me handle this,' Ozzy said, stepping in front of Meg and clearing his throat. 'Focus to shut out everything but what lays before, intent to follow through on that which she has committed to, and concentration on the spell itself.'

'Blimey, Fluffy, you sound like one of them 'ere dictionaries,' Boo said, then laughed.

'My name is Ozzy.' Ozzy glared at Boo through his slitted yellow eyes before putting his nose in the air and stalking off.

'But we didn't see any of that, Meg. You were just humming to yourself as you walked,' Mina pointed out.

'I was, but my mind was on creating something special for you so—'

'So, inadvertently you did what Gertie and the Coven have been trying to get you to do for ages… FIC,' Ozzy huffed, snubbing Boo again.

'You needn't fink you're botherin' me, Fluffy.'

'Boo,' Zoe warned.

'Anyway,' Mina interrupted, 'you said something about "most of it had followed". What do you mean?'

'Well, the rest is more about the stone releasing its pent-up energy,' Meg said and winked before she and Ozzy wandered a distance away. 'Are you ready?' she called.

Zoe, Mina and Boo looked at each other, before turning to Meg and nodding, a frisson of excitement tickling Mina's belly. 'Shouldn't we wake Achoo though?'

'Oh, he'll wake up soon enough.' Meg grinned and then turned her back. Ozzy wrapped himself around her legs.

Mina watched as Meg turned her face to the sky, spread her arms wide and began to chant. She couldn't hear what Meg was saying, but after a few moments, hearing words was not what Mina was focused on. Instead, she stared, her eyes widening at the glowing violet aura that surrounded Meg, pulsating quicker and quicker, the ground trembling as it did so.

'W-what's going on?' Achoo said, rubbing his eyes as he swiped an unwelcome branch off himself.

'Look!' Zoe hissed, pointing towards Meg.

'Whoooooa,' Achoo said.

'Far out,' Zoe stated.

'Not as good as them in 'ole London town,' Boo chimed.

'Magical,' Mina said, the colourful fireworks shooting from the magic stone around Meg's neck reflecting off her glasses. Her pupils were as wide as they could be to take in the brightness of the stars, because that's what they were— stars. 'Oh, Meg,' Mina said. 'You are a genuine witch.'

As Mina finished speaking, the fireworks died, and the wood returned to its quiet wakefulness.

'D-do you mean that?' Meg's small voice barely reached Mina's ears.

'Of course I do. Look at what you've done for us, instinctively,' Mina said as the smaller girl stood before her, tears running down her cheeks, a broad grin decorating her dimpled face.

'I did, didn't I?'

'Yes, you did,' Zoe said, draping her arm across Meg's shoulders. 'All you needed was to believe in yourself.'

'I don't fink that was it. I fink she believed in what she wanted to do. I fink that's the key,' Boo said and patted Meg's arm.

'Whatever it was, it was awesome,' Achoo said, wide awake for a change.

'I think you are all correct,' said Ozzy. 'But it's nothing myself and Gertie haven't been telling her for an age.'

'Yes, but, this time I wanted to do it… to thank my… friends… for helping me today,' Meg said, smiling shyly at each of them.

'Of course we're your friends, aren't we?' Mina said.

'Most definitely,' said Zoe.

'Yup,' Boo agreed.

'Deffo,' added Achoo.

'What's wrong?' Mina asked as she watched Meg's smile vanish and a dark cloud pass over her eyes.

'But Auntie Gert… she can never find out what happened today… promise?'

'Your secret is safe with us, Meg. Don't worry,' Mina said.

'Pinky swear,' Zoe said, holding out her little finger.

'Pinky swear.' Mina locked fingers with Zoe.

Boo and Achoo followed suit before they all turned to look at Meg.

'P-pinky swear,' Meg said, joining in, her tears and smile returning at full force.

'What about me?' Ozzy complained as he prowled around the group.

'I already know you'll never tell,' Meg said, scooping him up and burying her face in his fur. Ozzy made a show of pushing her away, but his loud purrs gave him away, and they all burst out laughing.

'Well, as much as I hate to be a party pooper, we—'

'Yeah, course you do, Fangless,' Boo said and rolled his eyes.

'I do! I'm having just as much fun as the rest of you, but time is marching on and we need to get back before school finishes.'

'Oh, before we go, I have something I need to do.' Meg wandered away from the group, Ozzy at her heels.

Mina watched with curiosity as Meg pulled something from her pocket, then turned her face to the sky and spread her arms again. This time, though, Mina didn't see the glow from the magic stone; its power back under control.

What are you up to, Meg? Mina mused.

***

Meg hummed to herself as they all made their way back to school.

'What are you so happy about?' Ozzy asked as he slunk along beside her, unable to stop his head bobbing to the cheerful tune.

'Oh, you'll see,' she said and ruffled his fur.

The others were ahead of her. Zoe was the furthest to make sure the coast was clear and they could slip back into the school grounds unnoticed. Achoo was ambling along, hands thrust deep into his pockets, his head down, paying little attention to his journey. Mina was conducting a conversation with someone. At first Meg thought it was Boo, but he didn't seem to be paying any attention, instead flitting between everyone, trying to make them jump. Needless to say, it wasn't working. All he did was get batted away like an irritating insect.

'I wonder who Mina's talking to?' Meg said to Ozzy.

'Anyone's guess with that one, and it wouldn't surprise me if it's herself.'

'Mmmm.' Meg went back to humming and grinned as she giggled.

'Come on, share. You always tell me,' Ozzy grumbled.

'I know, but—'

'You were casting another spell, weren't you, before we left?' Meg hadn't noticed Mina fall back in step with her and Ozzy.

'Oh, err…'

'I know you were. I'm curious to know what, though.' Mina put her hand on Meg's arm and the two of them stopped. 'It won't get you in any trouble, will it?'

Meg looked into the concerned eyes of her new friend and shook her head. 'No, I don't think so. Mind you, it will depend on how long it lasts for, as other than Auntie Gert, I am the only other witch in the school, so it wouldn't take them long to work it out.'

'I told you not to do anything,' Ozzy said.

'I know, but it will be worth any punishment I might get. Trust me.'

'You do know you're not supposed to use your magic to cause any harm,' Ozzy said.

'Oh, I know, and I'm not hurting anyone… not really.'

'What have you done?' Mina asked, her hand tightening on Meg's arm.

'Wait and see,' Meg said and winked, before hurrying to catch up with the others. Mina and Ozzy had no choice but to follow.

***

'Okay, we've got five minutes before the bell goes, so quick, everyone, we don't want it to be obvious we've been missing,' Zoe hissed as she ushered them all through the gap in the railings they'd sneaked out through, what seemed like hours earlier.

''Old your 'orses, Skater Girl, we'll get there,' Boo said, drifting over the top of the railings as only he could.

'Well, if you want to join Jonas and Griff in detention, be my guest,' Zoe said, 'But I don't.'

The friends hovered beside the main school building, ready to merge with the throng of students as they raced out once the bell rang.

'So, are you going to tell us, or not? Our parents will be waiting and we'll need to leave,' Mina urged, her impatience clear as Meg watched her bobbing up and down on the spot, her gaze scouring the school yard for clues.

'Yes, do share,' Ozzy purred. 'Even I couldn't work out what you were doing, which is very unusual.'

'Come on, Meg, don't make us wait,' Zoe pleaded as she tried to remain in one place, her feet whizzing back and forth, making her look as if she was treading water in a pool.

'What's the big deal?' Achoo asked, then yawned. 'I'm looking forward to a little nap. I think I had too much cake.'

'Really, Wolfie, another sleep? That's not like you,' Boo teased.

Meg smiled and clapped her hands together. 'Okay, I'll tell you, but I'm not sure if you'll get to see anything until tomorrow.'

'Nothin' like bein' cryptic, is there?' Boo said, settling in to listen anyway.

'Well, I've kind of put a spell on Jonas,' Meg said, grinning from ear to ear as she looked at each of them.

'Oooo, what kind of spell? Is he going to grow frogs' legs?' Zoe asked, and laughed.

'Or donkey ears?' Achoo snorted, sneezing, but just managing to control his wolfing out.

'If she's got anythin' about 'er, she'll 'ave made him unpopular,' Boo added.

'No, just make him a victim for a change,' Mina finished, nodding.

Meg smiled at their ideas, patting Mina's hand. 'You're the closest, Mina. As punishment for taking my magic stone, I've made it so he can't touch anything.' Meg giggled, and Mina frowned.

'But how?'

'Well, after Zoe's clash with him, I snagged a hair from his head. He didn't notice as he was too busy fighting off snake Mina. Something like this is crucial to any spell which inflicts anything on a person.'

'So, how have you made it so he can't touch?' Zoe asked.

'Because everything he does touch will be so hot, he won't be able to hold on to it.' Meg smiled smugly as she stroked Ozzy.

'And how long is this spell of yours going to last for, as it sounds to me like you'll be found out soon enough?' he said.

'Until he learns what it feels like to be vulnerable,' Meg said, her smile disappearing as she remembered how Jonas had made her feel that day.

'Well, that's something he's never felt in his life,' said Mina, 'So that could take a while.'

The door to the sports hall banged open, distracting Meg, and she gasped, clamping her hand over her mouth to stifle a guffaw. She cleared her throat, pressed her lips together to compose herself, and then grinned again. 'I don't think so,' she said and nodded towards the sports hall.

Boo, Mina, Achoo, Zoe and Ozzy all turned to watch

Jonas slinking from the building, a dark stain decorating the front of his trousers.

They all gasped and turned to look at Meg, their mouths agape.

Meg shrugged. 'And now the spell is broken.'

Boo was the first to erupt in laughter, but soon they all joined in. Achoo rolled around on the floor, his hands clutching his belly.

Mina was the first to compose herself. 'Okay, everyone, I think we should stop now.'

'Aw, come on, Fangless, that is legend.'

'Yes, I agree, but it isn't right to laugh at someone else's misfortune.'

'It is after what he's done,' Zoe said.

'No bad deed goes unpunished, as my dad likes to say,' Achoo piped up as he lay spread-eagled on the ground.

'I think you let him off a bit too lightly, Meg, if I'm honest,' Zoe continued. 'I have many things I can think of that would be more fitting. You could—'

'It's a good job Meg is a white witch then, isn't it?' Mina interrupted, fixing Zoe with a stern look over the top of her glasses.

'You are sooooo boring sometimes,' Zoe grumbled.

At that moment the bell rang. The thunder of feet followed close behind.

'Well, I think that's our cue,' Meg said, turning to face the friends. 'Unfortunately, as Auntie Gert gave Jonas detention, I've got to sit through it too.'

'I think you mean "we",' Ozzy corrected.

'Okay, we've got to sit through it,' Meg said, picking Ozzy up.

'Promise me you'll continue to torment Jonas,' Zoe said, a wicked look in her eyes.

'Mmmm, I may have a few small things planned, 'Meg said and winked.

'That's the spirit,' Boo said. 'Don't let 'im off too lightly.'

'Before you go,' Meg said as they all turned to leave, 'I-I just wanted to thank you for today… you know… for helping me get my magic stone back. I don't know what I'd have done if…' Meg didn't finish, her voice catching in her throat as fresh tears caught her off guard.

'That's what friends are for,' Mina said.

'Anyway, I think you've thanked us enough, hasn't she, Achoo?' Zoe said.

Achoo gave a thumbs up from his position on the ground.

'Friends,' Meg said, a warm glow spreading through her body, causing her to hug Ozzy a little too tight for his liking. 'Ouch! What was that for?' Meg dropped Ozzy, rubbing her chest where he'd sunk his claws to express his discomfort.

'Right, I think we should go. I can see my mother's car, and she *so* does not like to be kept waiting,' Mina said. 'See you all tomorrow.'

The others responded the same and Meg waved as her new friends left for the day. Then she trudged inside the school building, a glint in her eye as to the small things she could do to Jonas during detention.

School's Out

'What's the matter with you?' Achoo's dad asked as he dropped into the passenger seat. His dad grabbed his chin and forced Achoo to look him in the eyes. 'You look exhausted. Don't tell me you've been struggling to control your wolfing out again?' He let go and Achoo massaged his chin as his dad started the car and pulled away from the curb.

'Well?' his dad prompted.

'Well, what?'

'Have you been struggling to control your wolfing out?'

Achoo pondered how best to answer the question, but found no other way than the truth. 'Yes,' he said and shrugged.

'For goodness' sake, Achoo, we've been working on this. How can this still be a problem?' his dad demanded, slapping his palm against the steering wheel, making Achoo jump.

'In my defence, it was deliberate.'

'How can you deliberately not control your wolfing out?'

'Because I needed to do it to help track down a missing… object…'

Achoo decided it best not to add in the bit about the object being stolen, knowing his dad would have launched into a long complaint about the standards in the school. Achoo liked school, well, as much as anyone could, and didn't want to be made to leave and go to the stuck-up school across town. He wanted to stay with his friends.

'A friend had lost something precious to her and my

super sense of smell, which you know is always better when I am a werewolf, helped find it.'

Achoo glanced at his dad, whose gaze was fixed on the road ahead, his jaw working as though he was chewing a particularly difficult sweet.

After what seemed an age, his dad glanced at him quickly before turning back to the road.

'In that case, Achoo, I'm very proud of you. Well done for helping your friend, and for remembering to use your senses to the best of their ability.'

***

Mina slid into the back of the sleek black limousine and immediately pressed the button to lower the window, angling her face towards the sun.

'Vladmina! How many times have I told you about how bad that… that… thing is for your skin? Close that window at once.' Mina sighed, but obeyed her mother, slouching back against the seat and crossing her arms. She ran her tongue over her teeth, her heart lurching as she found the gaps.

Oh no.

Mina patted her pocket. The fangs were still there. Turning her body away from her mother, Mina retrieved her prosthetics and was pushing one into place when her mother spoke.

'What are you doing?'

'N-nothing,' Mina said, her mouth open as she tried to get her fang in the right position.

'Are you by any chance putting in your prosthetics?'

Mina stopped what she was doing and turned to face her mother. 'Um, nope.'

'Open your hand.'

Mina tried to push the remaining tooth underneath her, but her mother's hand shot out, grabbing her wrist and dragging her hand forward. Mina squeezed her fist tightly.

'Vladmina, look at me.' Reluctantly, Mina dragged her gaze to meet her mother's in the gloomy interior of the car. 'Open you hand… now.'

Mina clenched her teeth, willing her body not to respond, but as always, her mother's powers of persuasion proved too great.

'What have I told you about wearing these at all times?' her mother snapped as she grabbed the tooth from Mina's palm. 'Open your mouth.'

Again, Mina had no choice but to obey, and her mother thrust the remaining fang into position, bringing tears to Mina's eyes.

'I do not want to see you without them again. Do I make myself clear?'

Mina nodded, not trusting her voice as she brushed the stray tears from her cheeks.

'Now, tell me about school. How much of your vampire nature has that school enabled you to use today, since they're clearly not having much luck with your attire?'

Mina bit her tongue, swallowing down her normal retort when her mother criticised her choice of clothing.

At least I wear things other than black.

'Actually, I was able to practise two things today,' she said instead.

'Oh really? I find that hard to believe, but do tell.'

Mina jabbed the button for the window, allowing it to open a few inches before she replied.

'Well, I did. I used my mind-reading to help a friend remember exactly what she'd been doing before she discovered she'd lost something important. Then I morphed into… I morphed to help retrieve the object once we'd tracked it down.'

'Really, darling? You read someone's mind? Oh, you have no idea how happy that makes me,' her mother said and reached out to run her blood-red nails along Mina's jawline.

And you have no idea how happy I am you haven't asked what I morphed into, Mina thought.

※ ※ ※

'Zoe Mort, what on earth have you been doing?' Zoe's mum gasped when Zoe skidded to a halt in front of her.

'Nothing unusual,' Zoe said and shrugged, handing her backpack to her mum.

'Nothing unusual? Then how are you in such a state? Look at your arm.' Mrs Mort grabbed hold of Zoe to keep her still and cast an appraising look over every inch of her. Zoe, in true Zoe form, fidgeted under her mum's scrutiny. 'Your ankle, too. Do you want to be laid up while I get the doctor in to repair you?'

'Ugh, no.' Zoe screwed her face up, remembering the last time she'd been in that position, after losing her head.

'Well then, you need to take better care of yourself. I don't know how many times I've told you, duct tape can only do so much.'

'Yeah, yeah, I know.'

'Then why don't you listen to me?'

'I do listen, Mum. I can't help it if accidents happen or I have to pull myself apart to help someone.'

'You had to do what?' her mum asked, holding fast to Zoe as she tried to skate away. 'What did you do and, more to the point, why?'

'Let go of me and I'll tell you.' Zoe held her mum's stare until her mum let go and Zoe promptly zoomed off.

'Zoe Mort, a deal is a deal,' her mum called, and Zoe rolled her eyes.

Some people have no patience.

After a few laps around her mum, Zoe stopped and linked arms instead, rolling in time with her mum's shuffling steps.

'Well, a friend had lost something important, and she was so upset about it, she locked herself in the toilet cubicle and wouldn't come out. All I could do was take myself apart to slide under the door and talk to her.'

'Did it work?'

'Oh yes, as did my speed… again.'

'I find that very hard to believe,' her mum grumbled.

'Well, it did. We had a plan and my part was to zoom in and retrieve the lost object when the chance arose.'

'And do I want to know the details of this plan?'

'Not really. All you need to know is that me, Mina, Boo and Achoo helped Meg, our new friend, get back what she'd lost.'

'Hmmm. I'll take your word for it.' Zoe's mum gave Zoe a stern look before they shuffled off into the sunset.

***

Boo sauntered towards his parents, his mam smiling broadly, his dad frowning as always. He braced himself for the inevitable question… and wasn't disappointed.

''Ow you getting on wi' learnin' 'ow to scare folk?'

'Oh, Jack, leave him alone, he's only just got out,' his mam said, giving Boo a hug and peppering his face with kisses.

'Maaam!' Boo shrugged away and wiped her slobber from his face.

'Aren't I allowed to miss my boy?'

'Edith, not now,' his dad said. 'Tell me, Boo, 'ave you scared anyone today?'

Boo cast his mind back to his tickling of Griff. He hadn't exactly scared him, although Griff had acted like he was.

'Umm, I did make meself disappear—'

'That's 'ardly difficult at your age—'

'Let him finish, Jack.'

Boo looked from his mam to his dad, who gritted his teeth before giving a curt nod.

'I then kept me focus an' I scared the Adam and the Ants outta someone to 'elp get back a lost… er… object.'

'Are you telling me the Babe Ruth, boy?'

'Course, I am, Dad. I wouldn't tell you a pork pie.'

His dad harrumphed, while his mam put her arm around him and hugged him close.

''Ow did it make you feel, you know, scarin'?'

Boo pondered this. He had actually quite enjoyed it. Probably because it was Griff, but he didn't need to tell his dad that.

'Pretty good,' he said and grinned.

'I told you, didn't I? Best feelin' in the world, scarin' folk.'

His dad put his arm around Boo's shoulders, too.

'Also, you know 'ow I likes to 'ave a natter? Well, that 'elped find this lost object too.'

Boo felt his dad's arm drop from his shoulders and he chanced a look up and saw his dad's frown. He grinned and shrugged before the family drifted off towards home.

***

The Misfits go to bed happy in the knowledge they saved Meg from getting into trouble for something that wasn't really her fault.

We all lose things, and what is important is having those things returned to us by the person who finds them. After all, you never know how precious and irreplaceable the item you've found might be to the owner. Think about how you would feel if you lost the thing you value most in the world and someone else found it, but wouldn't give it back to you.

The Misfits have also made a new friend today, a friend they know they'll be seeing a lot more of in the future.

THE END

Reviews are my life blood

As an indie author, it isn't just about writing a fantastic story that leaves you, dear reader, wanting more; I am also a one-woman publishing house—Scarygirl Ltd.

Being a publisher as well as an author means I have to pay for an editor, proofreader, and cover designer out of my own pocket. And then there's formatting, marketing, advertising, and distribution of physical copies to bookstores.

For me to succeed in the world of indie writing and publishing, I have to have the support of a great team, and I do.

And you, dear reader, are a vital part of my team.

To continue to write and publish the stories you love, I need to get word out about my books, and **reviews** are one of the best ways to achieve this.

So, team member, I am asking for your help.

If you enjoyed this book, it would mean the world to me if you would leave a review on Goodreads, your favourite reviewing spot, or on the site where you bought this book.

Thank you so much for reading my tales and for supporting me.

About the Author

M. A. COPE is the pen name of author Marie Anne Cope, who lives in North Wales with her three cats and has been, at various times, a banker, auditor, yoga teacher, and a radio presenter. Marie is the author of the BONDS and TALES FROM A SCARYGIRL series. THE MISFITS & THE MAGIC STONE is the second volume in THE MISFITS series.

You can reach Marie at geni.us/MarieAnneCope
www.facebook.com/MarieAnneCopeAuthor
www.instagram.com/marieannecopeauthor

Acknowledgements

I penned The Misfits and The Magic Stone soon after I'd finished The Misfits, but other projects took over. When Achoo, Mina, Zoe and Boo jumped up and down and insisted I share Meg's story with the world, I thought I best do as they asked!

Meg's story is a pertinent one, after all, who as kids heard the rhyme: 'finders keepers, losers weepers'? When I was young, I heard it all the time when I dropped something and someone else picked it up. It was horrible, especially when that item was precious to me. I think it is important for everyone, especially children, to learn that when you find something you must try the best you can to return that item to its rightful owner because, as in Meg's case, you don't know how important it might be.

My utmost thanks go to the forever talented Jonathan Brier for bringing Meg, Ozzy, Jonas and Griff to life and joining them with Achoo, Mina, Zoe and Boo on this amazing cover. I would also like to thank my editor, Steven Moore, for reviewing my scribblings and highlighting where I could make improvements.

Most of all, though, I would like to thank you, dear reader, for your patience in waiting for The Misfits' next adventure and for spending your hard-earned pocket money on this book. I hope you enjoyed it.

Printed in Great Britain
by Amazon

24031504R00056